OUR FATHER'S FOOTSTEPS

BY C. S. HOBSON

TABLE OF CONTENTS

CHARACTERS

PREFACE

Although the characters and events in this book are loosely based on actual people and events it is a work of fiction. The story is true to life, and things contained in it did happen in some way shape or form at some point, but the names were changed and the order and timing of events were manipulated and slightly altered to fit the storyline. Life imitates art and art imitates life.

DEDICATION

I would like to dedicate this book to the people in my life who have had the biggest influence on me and without whom I would not be who I am today. My parents, Lawrence and Cynthia Hobson, whose love, inspiration, and belief in me has inspired me to always do my best in whatever I do, and who always showed such faith and confidence in me and what I could achieve in life.

My brothers Bryan and Chris have always been my heroes in their own distinctive and unique ways. My beautiful wife Lola for her understanding and for being the rock that studies me and keeps me grounded, and who is by far the better half of our partnership. My step daughter Cynthia, son in law David, and my grandkids, Marcello, DJ, JuJu, and Alexis, my sister-in-law Karen, my nieces Shelby, Korryn and Olivia, my nephews Justin and Isaiah, and Justin's wife Ahirlee. I thank all of you for love and support. I would also like to thank my Nana, who blessed us all with her love and support, and whose unwavering commitment to her family is still felt by all of us today.

All of these people played a huge a part in inspiring me to continue on my journey to complete this book and I would like to thank each and every one of them for their support and for their love.

Searching for truth can be a two edged sword.

On one hand it can be liberating,

Sobering

Satisfying to our souls,

And on the other hand it can be stinging

Painful and leave us with a bitter taste in our mouths.

It can stir up many different emotions in our pursuit of it

And,

We don't really know how we will feel once we do find and confront it

One thing is certain however,

The truth is what it is .

We can try to hide it,

We can try to dance around it

We can try to manipulate it,

Dispute it

And even try to spin it to look like something else

But

We can never change it

And

 If in pursuit of it

We happen to find it

We must accept it

For it is what it is and it can never be changed

THE CALL

It was just around midnight when the loud ringing of the telephone awakened me from my blissful and well deserved sleep. I was exhausted from a long and crazy day at work and I'd just dozed off. As I clumsily reached to pick up I remember thinking it had to be one of three things, a wrong number, someone calling with bad news, or, maybe a booty call. It's a crapshoot, and the way things had been going for me I was pretty sure that it wasn't the latter, so I was really hesitant to pick it up. I always had hope though, so when I picked up I said what I always said

"What up!"

There was no answer. All I could hear on the other end was the faint sound of music and voices in the background, as though the call was coming from a bar or a nightclub or something. I said hello again, a little louder this time, probably sounding irritated at being awakened at such a late hour, and after a few more seconds I started to hang up. Finally, someone on the other end said something back

"Perry, is that you?"

I sat up in my bed still trying to clear my head. I could barely hear the voice on the other end. I could however hear that it was a man's voice which meant that it wasn't the booty call that I'd hoped for, so my interest in what this person had to say went away pretty quickly. The person spoke again

"What's up P, it's Caesar"

Still not knowing who it was, I angrily shouted into the phone

"Caesar, Caesar who?"

This time the voice answered right away, in a somewhat louder tone this time

"It's me Caesar Martinez"

Anger and confusion immediately filled my mind. This couldn't be possible. Why was this punk calling me? I would have thought I would be one of the last people he would want to talk to, let alone call at 12:00 midnight. Plus, I thought he was still locked up. The last time I'd seen him was at his trial, and at that time he couldn't even look me in the face. The last words I heard out of his mouth on that day were him admitting what he'd done, before the judge announced his sentence. He'd pleaded guilty to manslaughter as part of a plea bargain. I swore to myself that day if I ever laid eyes on him again I would kill him for what he'd done, and now here it was seven years later and he is calling my phone.

I stood up and screamed into the phone.

"Are you fucking kidding me? How the hell did you get my number and why are you calling me?"

After a few seconds of silence he answered
"I'm calling because I have no one else to turn to or that can help me."

Barely able to control my emotions by this time, I snapped back at him
"Help you, what the fuck makes you think I would ever want to help your punk ass? If you were here right now I would choke the life out of you."

Again he answered
"I just thought you would want to know who really killed Corey."

What the hell was he talking about? I already knew who'd killed Corey, him, he'd admitted it in an open courtroom.

Before I could say anything, he continued on.

"I swear on my family Perry, I didn't kill Corey. I spent the last seven years of my life in prison for something I didn't do, and now I know who did it. I also know why it was done. Would you please just meet me at the Touch Of Class over on Stockton Blvd. later tonight at around 7:00 p.m.? If you do I can prove to you that I am innocent, and if I can't and you don't believe what I have to say, I'll never bother you again."

He really had a lot of nerve asking me that.

After a moment of silence he continued

"Man P, I know you don't believe me, but what if I'm telling the truth, and there was someone else who did it, wouldn't you want to know who it was?"

What could he possibly have to tell me that I didn't already know? It was burned into my memory and changed me forever. It was obvious to everyone what happened, and who had done it. The only question on everyone's mind was why, why did he do it? He and Corey never had any real beef between them besides the fact that he really didn't like that Corey was dating his sister Carmen. He knew that their parents would have gone crazy if they'd ever found out. That wasn't a reason to kill him though, so when it happened, and he confessed to it everyone was as shocked as they were angry, especially because it was such a senseless crime that wounded the entire community very deeply.

Even though I still felt like I could kill him for what he'd done, my curiosity of what he had to tell me was overwhelming, and so I agreed to meet him.

"Ok, yeah, I'll meet you over at the Touch at around seven. But Caesar, there is something that I want to make very clear to you before I meet you so listen to me very carefully. If I don't like or believe what you have to say, I promise you on everything that I hold dear to me you won't make it out of there. I just want to make sure that you understand that."

Sounding relieved, he quickly responded,

"I understand and it's a risk I'm willing to take, thanks P."

After I hung up, I began to think back on what happened those seven years ago, and as I slowly drifted back to sleep, I dreamt of it as if it were happening all over again. It was a nightmare none of us would ever wake up from, and that would change all of our lives forever.

As I showered and got ready to leave for work that next morning I couldn't stop thinking how Caesar had to have a huge set of balls to call and ask me to meet him. Feelings of anger continued to flow through my veins and the hate I had for him grew stronger and stronger. By the time I was ready to leave the house to go to work the anger inside had gotten so strong that I almost called in sick just so I could avoid whatever it was that was going to happen that night.

Anger is an emotion that I have always had a great deal of control over until someone or something takes me to that point that we all reach if we get angry enough, or, if something irritates me to a point where I can no longer control myself or what I am doing. When I reach that point it is not pretty, and I try my best to keep myself out of situations where I get to that point because it's usually not good for whatever or whoever the source of my anger comes from - not very pretty at all. I lose complete control of myself. This was one of those situations. Deep down inside however, I knew I had to meet Caesar. I needed to know what he had to tell me. The curiosity was eating me up all day. I had no way of knowing however, that meeting would change the course of my life and the lives of all of the people involved in what happened those seven summers ago on that hot night in August, a senseless murder of a beautiful innocent teen that would change my life and the lives of my friends forever.

THE SUMMER OF 1980

Cotton in the Sky

I used to kick back in the grass and let the world go by,
I'd just lay back and watch the clouds of cotton in the sky
I'd block out all the noise, silence was every place,
And gentle winds would softly blow the grass across my face
The skies were oh so blue then, the air so fresh and clean,
The sun was so much brighter then, the grass so soft and green
There was no stress or problems, no fear of things to come
There was no job or bills to pay, just endless days of fun
The funny thing is way back then I wanted to be grown
To stay up late, hang out with friends, and do things on my own
But now that I have grown, I miss the summers gone
Those golden days of kicking back and playing in the sun
I guess as we grow older we finally realize
That being young was not that bad and just how fast time flies
So in your youth enjoy your time, for it will soon fly by
And take the time to watch the clouds of cotton in the sky

My name is Perry Mason Nelson, and I was named after a lawyer on a TV show that was popular back in the early 1960s. From what my parents told me they were both huge fans of the series and I was named after the main character because they'd always hoped that I would grow up to be a famous lawyer one day just like the character in the show. That didn't happen however, and whenever they would bring it up I would just laugh it off and say, oh well, you get what you get, and they usually let it go after that. Sometimes I would go a little further with it and thank them for not naming me what they'd originally intended to before they came up with

Perry – Sherlock. That would have been an extreme act of cruelty and it would have made my life a living hell growing up.

I have two God given gifts, my ability to read people and my ability to solve problems or mysteries that most people can't. I use the term God given gifts because I truly believe that we are all given gifts from God when we are born, gifts that we are intended to use in our lives on the path that has been set out for us, to reach our fullest potential and purpose in life. That purpose is not meant to be one in which we do things just for the good of ourselves, but to also do things for the good of others. Most people however never really discover their gifts, or get lost along the path. Then there are those like myself, who, for whatever reason gets lost at many points on their journey down the path, but eventually make their way back at some point to continue along the road that they were meant to travel.

My ability to read people is the ability to tell whether a person is being honest with me by simply sitting down with them and having a candid conversation about their likes and dislikes, their jobs, their friends, their relationships, etc. I observe how they react to my questions and the answers they give and I can tell if they are telling me the truth or not. I don't mean to imply that I can read minds or anything like that, just that I have an uncanny ability to analyze a person's words and body language, and quickly determine who they are as a person and if they are being honest. It's really kind of spooky sometimes how I can do this with such accuracy, but without a doubt, I can.

Although my ability to read people has really come in handy in my life, I believe the stronger of my two gifts is my ability to solve problems, situations, or mysteries that most people feel are impossible to solve. This gift has been of great help to me in both my work and in my personal life. It can get a little tricky sometimes to navigate through a situation and to tell how things will go and if in using my gifts I am being helpful to people, or, if it will cause them harm. It is a very thin line that usually comes down to finding out what the truth is, and then letting fate determine where I go from there. This approach would serve me well as me and my friends attempt to solve the mystery of events that occurred that summer, the summer in which all of us would be forced to leave the innocence of our youth and face what can be a cold and harsh transformation into becoming young adults.

The year was 1980. It was early August, and it was going to be another of the many scorching hot 100 degrees plus days in Sacramento that year. It was a beautiful Saturday morning and the temperature had already reached around 90 degrees by 10:00 am. I didn't care though. Even if it got up to 110 that day, it wouldn't matter because this was the day that me and my boys were going to handle our business and take those busters from the north side to school. The park was going to be packed with people that day. More specifically, it was going to be packed with pretty young babes wearing short tight skirts and low cut tops, all trying to escape the heat swimming at the pool, or by chilling under the trees while watching us play ball. Those Marks didn't know what they had gotten themselves into but they were about to find out.

I had to wear my new white leather, high top Doctor J's, with the purple Converse symbol on the side, that my parents had just bought me for the school team. It was going to be my senior year and my last year and all of the guys on the team would be wearing them. My pops would have killed me if he knew I was going to wear them outside and he'd warned me that I'd better take care of them or I would be running around playing in my socks because he wasn't buying me any more. I don't think he really meant it but I didn't want to find out. This however, was a special occasion, so I wore them that day along with my white tank top and my purple and white gym shorts that matched the shoes. I had to be matching and everything had to be fitting just right.

As I finished putting on my shoes I looked over at my brother and asked him if he was coming up to the park with us to play against the north side dudes that had challenged us the day before.

"Na, I have to do my homework"
Who's going? "

"Me, Juju, Q, and Corey"

"Who are the north side dudes bringing to play?"

I really didn't know, but I wanted to entice him to play, so I threw out a few names of players he'd played against on the school team to see if it would make him want to go. I knew if I could get him to play with us we would be a lock to win. We never lost when we all played together, ever.

We played basketball in our backyard all day everyday and knew each others games so well that when we played we were like a well oiled machine. I honestly don't remember us ever losing. After I mentioned the player's names I thought might entice him to go, he hesitated for a few minutes, and then after giving it some thought he said,

"I have to get this work done."

Disappointed I headed for the door

"Ok that's cool. I'll see you later. Are you sure?"

"Yeah, I might go up there later."

So I still had hope. Justin, or Ace as we called him, was always into school first. No matter what, he had to make sure his homework was done before he did anything else. I was into school also but not as much as him. At the time I didn't understand his passion for education and thought it was kind of square for him to be so much into it, and at that time it really used to irritate me. It wasn't until we got older that I came to understand and admire his dedication and commitment to school, and how important it is for young people to be leaders and not followers, and to not take school for granted. At that time though I didn't really understand why he would rather stay home and do homework instead of going up to the park with us and putting a ass whoopin on these boys in front of all those girls and people, but even though it frustrated me at the same time I admired him for it if that makes any sense.

As I walked out the front door and on to the porch I could see and smell the steam rising from the newly laid tar that had been put on our street the day before. The street looked great, but it smelled terrible. As I walked out to the sidewalk I could see Juju and Q walking down the street towards me dribbling their balls. As they approached I could hear them talking about something but I couldn't quite make out what it was until they got close enough for me to hear. The Waters boys, Andrew, aka Juju, and Quincy, aka Q, were the first two kids we met when we first moved to 33rd Street from my grandmother's house. Their parents, Harold and Loraine Waters had moved to the neighborhood several years before us, and they welcomed our family with open arms as soon as we moved on the street. They had a huge family of 11 kids of various ages. Juju was Ace's age, Q was my age, and their younger brother Stephen or Steph was my younger brother Tone Tone's age. After we moved to 33rd, we quickly became best friends, and we all did everything together, I mean everything. Most of all we all excelled in football, baseball, and basketball. We all loved to play basketball the most however, and we would play all of the time. We had a basketball hoop in our backyard and the Waters boys would come over pretty much everyday, rain, cold, heat, day and night, and play on our backyard court, as did all of the kids on our block. That is how we all got so good and skilled at hoops and how we learned how to play so well together. It's funny how kids today spend most of their time inside playing games on their computer or PS4's, or, when they are outside, looking at their phones. We played outside from sun up to sun down until my mom had to come out and call for us to come in. Sometimes she would have to come and get us, but we didn't want that because that could turn out bad for us. Anyway, that was how we met and became best friends with the Waters boys.

As they got closer to me I could finally hear what they were talking about. It was an incident that we were all very familiar with. Juju asked if Ace was coming and I said no. He looked at Q, punched him in the arm and said

"I thought you said Ace was coming"

Juju usually didn't want to play with us unless Ace was playing. Q swung back at him, missed and said

"P told me he was coming"

Juju hesitated for a minute as if he were thinking about not going, so I said that I'd heard there were a bunch of fine ass girls up at the park that day. After a few more minutes of hesitation, he agreed to go. So we started up 33rd street, crossed 12th avenue, and headed up toward the park.

On the way to the park, Q continued with what he was talking about when they were coming up to the house. It was regarding something that happened to a friend of ours named Marcello McFerrin who'd been killed by police officers the previous summer around this same time. Marcello, who was the oldest of the three McFerrin brothers, was a star pitcher from the time he was 10 years old, and as a freshman was a star on Sac high's baseball team. His brothers, whose names were Stevie and Bruce, were also very good at baseball and played in the Oak Park Little League. Baseball would be Marcello's ticket to success. Everyone said he was a natural, and would be a star pitcher one day. He always said he wanted to make it to the big leagues so that he could get his mom and his brothers everything that they always wanted but were unable to get. That was his sole motivation and he was well on his way. His father, Joseph or Jojo as he was known in the park, was in prison serving a 25 year bid for murder in commission of a robbery. When he went to prison Marcello was eight years old, and it left him, his two brothers and their mother, Barbara, alone, and to fend for themselves.

Times were very tough for them, and to make ends meet Barbara worked two jobs, one as a janitor at Sutter Middle school, and the other as a maid for a family over in Fair Oaks. She would leave the house each morning to work both jobs and not return home until around 9:00 p.m. Each day before leaving she would always tell her boys that she loved them, to be careful, and to make sure they were home before it got dark. She would also warn them to stay away from the park.

That evening, Barbara was working late after being asked to work a few hours extra at her second job in Fair Oaks. Despite their mother's warnings, Marcello and his two brothers went over to the park to play baseball and to hang out with friends before heading home at around 8:30 p.m.. It was starting to get dark around that time. As they walked down 34th street and were getting ready to pass the vacant lot by the Liquor store, a car pulled up in front of them blocking their path. Whoever was in the car shined a bright light on the three brothers and two white men dressed in suits jumped out of the car with guns in their hands and yelled for them to get on the ground. At that point, the boys, confused and scared to death, took off running back towards the park. They ran through the park and the baseball field and towards the other end which was lined by the backyards of the homes that were on the Southside of the park.

The men with guns in hand were in hot pursuit of the boys, and were yelling at them to get their black asses on the ground or they were going to blow their heads off. The three brothers, who were ages 13, 15 and 16, either didn't hear the men, who later said they identified themselves as police officers, or did not believe them, continued to run towards the houses.

As they reached the fence of one of the backyards they all went to jump over the fence and into the yard, thinking that if they made it over the fence they were home free. Marcello, after first helping his two younger brothers make it safely over the fence first, attempted to make it over himself. As he got to the top of the fence however, his pant leg got caught up in the top of the fence wire. He freed himself and went to jump to the ground on the other side, and just then two loud bangs rang out, echoing throughout the park. Two more shots quickly followed. Two of the bullets fired by the officers found their mark, hitting Marcello in his back. Marcello let out a scream and fell to the ground on the other side of the fence. As he laid there the two younger boys looked into their brother's eyes and they could see what they both later described as a look of fear, surprise, and extreme pain all rolled into one. He yelled

"They shot me"

He rolled on to his stomach and attempted to get up but he couldn't. They went to him to try and help him up, but he could not move, and though they wanted to stay with him, he yelled at them to go and get their mother.

"Go get momma"
"Quick, go and get momma"

The two boys quickly jumped to their feet and took off to get their mother who should have been home for work by that time.

The two men jumped over the fence and shined their flashlights on the person who they'd just shot, who was lying on his stomach with two holes in his back with thick blood flowing out of them. As they turned him over they said it was only then that they saw they had made a huge mistake, and that it was a teenage boy who they'd shot and not one of the people that had been robbing stores in the area over the past month.

Barbara had just gotten home from work and had changed into her robe and slippers, and was just getting ready to call out for her boys to come home. She figured they were down the block from the house or something and had lost track of time. As she opened the door to go out, Stevie and Bruce came running up to the door screaming

"Momma, "two white men just shot Marcello in the back! Hurry up, he told us to come and get you, hurry"

Barbara grabbed Stevie and asked him to repeat what he'd just said

"Two white men jumped out of a car and chased us. When we tried to jump over the fence, they shot Marcello and he told us to run and get you, come on momma hurry up"

Barbara screamed, "Oh my God," and quickly followed the boys, leaving the front door wide open. She ran as fast as she could to get to her first born son, her mind the whole time racing with thoughts of what could have happened, and praying to God aloud as she ran.

"Please God, let him be ok."
"Please God, let my baby be ok."

When she got to the scene there were several police cars there and people were all gathered around. As she approached the scene, she still couldn't see or hear Marcello's voice and she prayed that maybe the boys were wrong, and that he was ok. As she made her way through the crowd however pure shock and disbelief overtook her. Pain shot through her heart like a thunderbolt as she finally saw a figure laying in front of her with the paramedics frantically working on him.

Was she dreaming, having a nightmare that she would soon be waking up from? She slapped herself several times to see if she could wake up. This couldn't be real. As she finally reached the body lying there, she realized this wasn't a dream. She screamed out in pain.

"Marcello, what happened?"
"What did they do to you baby?"
"Marcello, baby, are you ok, please be ok."

As he lay there in a pool of blood, he regained consciousness for a moment, and seeing that his mother was crying, in a faint voice that she could barely hear, he said,

"Don't cry momma, I will be ok, please don't cry."

He then passed out again, but this time it would be for good. He would never wake up or speak another word. He was gone.

All Barbara could do was scream as loud as she could in anguish, as she fell to her knees beside him and gently picked up his head and laid it in her lap. They loaded him into the back of the ambulance, Barbara climbed in with him, and they took off for the hospital. No sirens, no lights, no speeding, just a long slow ride to the hospital to take his body to the coroners to determine his cause of death.

But they didn't need a coroner to do that. Everyone already knew. After just hanging out in the park with their friends for the evening, walking, kicking the breeze, probably talking about things that all teenage boys talk about at that age, girls, cars, movies, life, whatever, enjoying a nice warm summer night without a care in the world, he was gone, dead at 16 years of age, gunned down for no reason other than the familiar one that everyone in Oak Park or any other black neighborhood in America knew too well, being a young black man in the wrong place at the wrong time. It turned out the teens looked nothing like the people who had been robbing stores in the area. What a surprise.

Q continued to tell us that the officers, who were put on probation at the time pending further investigation, were recently found not be guilty of any charges and to have been acting in accordance with police regulations and procedures. We couldn't believe it, but we were not really surprised because we had heard similar stories from time to time in the past. Kids were always warned by parents that when in the park, things like that could happen; and to never be out late at night walking the streets, because there were some police officers who were not there to protect and serve. They were there to harass and intimidate. Unfortunately, it was these types of officers, who were more plentiful at the time that made it tough for the major portion of good officers. It was tough for us to tell the difference between the two however, and it was safer and easier, in our eyes, to not trust any of them.

As we drew closer to the park, we began to see the sights and hear the sounds that could always be seen and heard on a hot summer day in the middle of August when the park was at its fullest and busiest. Huge oak trees outlined the entire park, and as you entered it they seemed to come alive. You could see and hear the crap games being played to the left, the voices of little kids in the kiddy pool which was filled to capacity, groups of older men at the far end socializing, drinking wine or whatever, arguing, conversing, little leaguers practicing over at the baseball fields, older kids and teens swimming at the big pool, groups of teens all over the place, and the basketball courts, full of street ballers, young, old, good, bad, all kinds were found there.

As we approached the courts I could see that the marks had actually shown up. I never thought they would, and they had brought their girls with them too. Not only had they dared to come over to the park, they were bold enough to think they had nothing to lose by doing so. They couldn't have been more wrong.

THE CHALLENGE

It all started on the day before, when Q and I decided to go and check out the new Bruce Lee movie at the State Theatre over by Florin Mall. Our plan was to catch the 82 bus to the movie and then walk across the street afterwards to cruise the mall and check out some girlies before heading home. The theatre was always packed during the summer with teens from all over Sacramento, and it was extra packed that day, which was great for us because the more packed it was the more girls there were for us to look at. It was so loud in there that day with people talking, you could barely hear the movie, but people didn't care much seeing as how most of them had come to get out of the heat, hang out and socialize. Bruce Lee movies were our favorites so when the three dudes in front of us began talking and laughing so loud that we couldn't hear a word of the movie, I asked them if they could keep it down a little so we could hear what was going on up on the screen. As they turned around, I could see that two of them were players on the Grant High basketball team on the North side of the city in Del Paso Heights. One of the guys from the team quickly said in a loud voice, "Hell no, we ain't gonna quiet down, especially for no punk ass fools from Sac High. " Everyone in the theatre got really quiet in anticipation of what would happen next. Some stood up to see, too. Instead of saying anything crazy back to them however, Q quickly said, "Man, I guess it's quiet enough to hear the movie now. "A loud sound of laughter came over the entire theatre, and for the moment, the tension that had been growing went down a few ticks. Everyone sat back down and watched the rest of the movie.

After the movie was over, we headed over to the mall to check out some girlies. When we got there, we ran into our other young homie Corey, who was there with his girl Carmen. Ever since he started seeing her, he never hung out with us anymore without her coming along. As we stopped and chopped it up with them for a few minutes, Q tapped me on the shoulder and pointed down the mall to the dudes who we'd had the issue with at the movies. They were standing there talking to three of the finest girls I had seen in the mall in a long time.

Q asked me, "You down?"
I said, "Yeah, I'm game".
Q asked Corey, You got our back?"
"For sho, you already know."

So with that, me and Q walked towards the group. As we walked past, Q looked at the girls, made sure they saw him, smiled, and we kept walking past, not too far though so they could still see us. As we stood there, I was able to get the attention of one of them, and I motioned for her to come over to us. She immediately did, of course, as did the other two girls, leaving those marks from the North side standing there looking like fools. As they walked up to us, I did like I always did and let Q take the lead in talking to them. I did this because even though my game was tight, Q had that next level game when it came to girls, and once he got it started, I could come in on the back end and help finish off the deal. Well, even though it turned out the girls were only schoolmates of theirs, I guess the Northsiders didn't appreciate the way we interrupted them when they were talking to them. So they walked over to us and started talking shit about Sac's basketball team and Oak Park. One of them said

"Ya'll aint even on our level when it comes to hoops. We could come over to the park and beat you on your own court."

By this time Corey had joined us in anticipation of something jumping off, and after hearing what they said, we all looked at each other and started laughing.

I asked "You got any money to back up all that shit you talking right now? Anyone can come up to the mall and talk shit about what they can and can't do, but we can't hear a word that's coming out of your mouth unless you got some money to back it up."

"Hell yeah, we got 50 bucks that says we can bring three of our home boys over to the park tomorrow, beat you on your own court, and then take your money"

I said "Cool! You got a game if you show up, but I don't think you will. I think you just sellin wolf tickets in front of these young ladies. Oh, and since you young ladies heard everything that we said, you have to come too so you can verify the terms of the bet."

They said they would come.

I said, "I guess we got a game then, twelve noon tomorrow, at the park. Come through, get that ass kicking, give us our money, and get the fuck up out of Dodge."

With that, the game was set. We would get Ace and Juju to go up to the park with me Q and Corey, handle our business, and get paid, and now we are here to collect.

As we approached the court where they were playing and saw the girls sitting on benches on the side of the court, I started to get hyped about the game. As I got closer, however, my excitement began to turn to concern as I could see the people who they'd brought to play. I felt a slight chill come over me, something wasn't on the up and up. They were trying to stack the deck. The two Mark's that we beefed with at the mall were there, but they'd also brought Michael Benz and Tony Jenkins with them. Michael Benz was first team all city and could fly just as high as Ace if not higher. Tony Jenkins (TJ), who had just finished his first year playing on scholarship at USC, could shoot the lights out. They were both part of their school's team that had made it to the State Final the previous Year. I felt a little sick. I knew we could probably hang with them, but with those two we were definitely a little outgunned, especially if Ace and Corey didn't show up. We couldn't back out now though, so as we approached the court, we began to look for some ballers from the park who we could pick up to kind of even things out.

When we arrived at the court, one of the marks, feeling pretty confident by now, said, "We thought ya'll wasn't gonna show up. You ready to run?

Where are your other two?" As I scanned the park, all I could do was hope and pray that the Lord would bless us this one time and have at least one of the real ballers show up to run with us. Suddenly I could see a slight worried look take over the previously confident expressions on the faces of our opponents. I then heard TJ say looking behind us, "Ok, now we got a game." When I turned around, a feeling of warm relief came over me. I saw Ace and the young phenom, DJ, walking up behind us. This was even better. Even though Corey flaked out on us, we had an even better squad with DJ. "Now we have a game!" I told the young ladies who were sitting on the side of the court. "You pretty young ladies just sit back, relax and watch this, because now we're going to take your boys to school." This was going to be a show. We shot for outs; we won and let them have the ball first.

The park had begun to come alive, and people, regular folks, old school and young ballers began to show up and crowd around the court. It was game time. It seemed as though everyone in the park, from the winos to the people shooting craps, to the hardcore thugs, stopped what they were doing to come over and check out the game. The game was to 16 by ones. Once we started to play it became extra physical, there was lots of shit talking right from the beginning. They were all very good players, and their skill level was much higher than I thought. It would definitely be a test for us and we would have to put out our A games to win. Hard fouls and no layups were the rules on both sides. The game swung back and forth with high flying dunks, 30-foot rainbow shots that rattled the chain nets as they went through, and the handles, oh the handles, especially from the freshman phenom DJ, brought loud cheers throughout the entire game. They actually went up on us 11-10 at one point and we could hear the crowd, especially the old school ballers that were watching the game, telling us we better not lose, and if we did, we couldn't come back to the park and play for the rest of the summer. I didn't know if they were serious about that, but I didn't want to find out.

It was our ball and Ace took the ball out and gave it to me, I took two dribbles and launched a 40 foot high arching rainbow jumper that hit the chains so hard that when it went through they came down and hit the pavement. I thought the ball had gotten wet because I shot it so high it had to have hit a cloud and brought some rain down or something. The game was tied at 11 and then something happened that I will never forget, and I still can't believe to this very day. DJ, the freshman phenom, perhaps spurred on by all of the talking that was going on, or bored and wanting to go do something else, put on a display of basketball skill and wizardry that I had never seen before or since from anyone in person. He began by stealing the ball at mid court, and then eluding three players while dribbling the ball behind him and moving forward at the same time. Once he had one foot in the key, he lifted off of the ground and went literally over the head of the defender in front of him, slamming the ball through the hoop with such force that the rim rattled for 10 seconds after that. Everyone jumped out of their seats and high fives were all over the place as cheers filled the air again.

It was 12-11 our favor. They came down and ran a pick play for what looked like an easy layup, when out of nowhere DJ came swooping in a like an eagle or a hawk or something and pinned the ball on the backboard, grabbed it, and took off to the other end like he was shot out of a cannon. He stopped on a dime at the free throw line, breaking two defenders' ankles, and elevated high in the air shooting a smooth as silk jumper that went straight through the hoop. It was 13-11 us at that point and after two more buckets by both sides, the score was 15-13 us and it was our ball with a chance to end the game.

It was time to run our play. The play that we worked and practiced on the long days and nights we all spent playing in our backyard. The play that up until that day we had never tried in a game for fear it may not work, and we would all be embarrassed for even trying it. But it was a hot and sticky summer day in August, we were in the park, our home court, it was packed, everyone was watching, including the honeys. If there was a perfect time to try it, now was the time. Q took the ball out and passed it to me. Ace set a screen for me at mid court and rolled off of it. Once I passed mid court, I waited for Q to set a screen for Juju who went around the screen toward to bottom of the key. Once he went off the screen, I looked DJ's way as if I were going to pass it to him and said "Here kill it DJ!" Instead of passing it to him however, I lofted a pass to Juju for a high-flying alley oop slam that he could have easily slammed through for the game winner. Instead of doing that however, he grabbed my pass with one hand and lofted it even higher to Ace who was coming from the other side of the key. As Ace grabbed the pass with both hands, TJ, who was standing right in front of the hoop, leaped high in front of the basket in an attempt to block the dunk. But it was too little to late, and Ace, seeing TJ jumping at the basket, seemed to continue to rise as he slammed it through the hoop backwards. Game over. The crowd went crazy!

Q having positioned himself right next to the main dude that had been doing all the talking, turned to him and said, "That's your draws punk, give me my money and get the fuck outa dodge."

We all stood there looking at each other as the guy actually acted like he didn't want to give up the money. I stepped up next to Q and then got up in the dudes face and said, "You heard what my home boy said. Give us our money and get the fuck outa dodge." "As a matter of fact, you can leave the girls here and we'll make sure they get home."

The guy looked at us and made the mistake of trying to save face by barking back, "We ain't giving ya'll nothing and we ain't going nowhere until we are ready to go."

It was about to be on. We had to get them then. It was the principal of the thing. Just then, both me and Q felt a hand on each of our shoulders kind of pushing us to the side. As we looked to see what was going on, Willie Boy Johnson walked between us and went straight up to the dude talking shit and put his face about 6 or seven inches away from him. Willie Boy's friends called him Buddha because he was huge and round, very light skinned, smoked weed so much his eyes always looked like they were half shut, and he was bald before being bald was cool. Only his friends could call him Buddha though, and if you didn't know whether he considered you a friend or not it would be smarter not to call him that.

Everything got quiet as Willie Boy said in a calm slow tone that sounded like half man and half angry pit-bull,

"You heard what my two little home boys said. Give them their money right now and get the fuck up outa here. As a matter of fact, after you break them off, break me off whatever you got left, and then I might let you get outa here without me kicking you and all of your home boys asses for even being around the park.

I actually started to feel sorry for the dude, but I didn't say anything because I didn't want to mess with Willie Boy myself. No-one did. He was the biggest, hardest, most dangerous thug in the park, at least for those who were our age. He wasn't even really worried about us getting our money as much as he saw this as an opportunity for him to get some money himself. The guy handed over his wallet, his gold chains, and his watch, and he and his boys quickly made it to their cars, and got up out of there as quickly as they could.

Q and I made it over to the girls who were all excited and scared at the same time. I asked them if they would like to hang out with us for a while before we took them home, and of course they said yes. We re-introduced ourselves to them and we hung out for the rest of the day. They were cool, and we chilled out with them kicking back, talking, laughing, and chilling for the rest of the day. The time flew by.

The next day was Sunday and they came by to pick us up to cruise through Land Park with them. This was one of many great weekends that I had as a youth growing up in Oak Park, a time in my life that I will always remember fondly as the golden times. I couldn't help wondering what happened to Corey though. He was a little younger than us, but he was very mature for his age and he would have never flaked on us and missed an important game like that. Never, that is, until he started seeing Carmen. She had his nose so wide open you could have driven a truck through it and still had room for a car coming in the opposite direction. That had to be what it was.

MURDER ON 10TH AVE

YOUNG LOVE

Young love is a tropical moonlit beach
On a warm dark summer's night
With a gentle breeze rustling the trees
And no one else in sight

It is a cold black tide that rolls in
Kissing the crystal shore
Gently cooling the burning sand
Only to disappear once more

It is a moonlit romantic scene
With stars shining so bright
It's a radio playing a jazzy tune
As romance fills the night

It is a faint hypnotic smell
Of perfume in the air
It is a gently chilled sex on the beach
For heat too strong to bear

It is two shadows that come together
And dance upon the sea
It is two hearts becoming one
Like they were meant to be

It is the story of young lovers
Dancing their very first dance
The mood is right and the scene is set
For passion and romance

It was 1979, and after a long and relatively boring summer, everyone was ready to get back to school. Corey, who had never really been into school prior to that year, decided over the summer that he was going to really put an effort into doing better in class and get better grades. He'd begun to figure out that he wasn't a little kid anymore and that in a relatively short period of time he would graduate from high school and be thrust into the world of young adulthood. This meant that he would have more responsibilities so he needed to start preparing himself for what life would bring him.

He arrived at home room early that day, and the first person that came in the room after him was Carmen. This however was not the Carmen that he'd seen on the last day of school just three months earlier. Although he'd always thought she was very cute, and worthy of a little game being shot her way, she had completely changed over the summer. Her skin, which had been slightly blemished, was clear and smooth, her hair, which was very short and lifeless just a few months before, was long and full of body. And speaking of body, she filled out her jeans and her halter top so well, much better than what he'd remembered from the last time he'd seen her.

Corey had also filled out over the summer. His long lean body, had become more muscular from working out with his brothers, and his squeaky little boy voice had deepened and sounded more like a young man. That is until he tried to speak to Carmen that day as she passed by his seat. As he tried to say hello, his voice temporarily went back and forth between his old squeaky little voice and his new deeper one. The normally talkative and flirty young man was tongue tied. When she smiled and spoke back to him, it was all over, he was hooked. He'd felt he was looking at an angel that had been sent down to earth, just for him. He couldn't take his eyes off of her for the whole time they were in home room that day, nor her off of him. He gave her his phone number and she said that she would call him later that day if she got the chance. She knew that it would be very difficult to do however, knowing her parents, and knowing the strict rules that they had for her as far as boys went. She had to try though. She had decided over the summer that she needed to live her own life and to do what she felt made her happy and not what they thought was best for her. Whether it was Corey or not, she wanted to experience life on her own terms and do things that she felt would make her happy. She wanted to meet people and friends that she liked being around, and meet and fall in love with whom she wanted.

When Carmen got home from school that day no-one was home yet, and wouldn't be for a while, so she thought it would be a good time to call Corey. Her palms were sweating as she dialed the numbers, partly because she'd never talked to a boy on the phone before, let alone called one, and partly because she was afraid that someone would walk in and catch her while she was talking to Corey. The phone only rang once and Corey, in anticipation of her call, quickly answered it. She was relieved that it was him that answered the phone, and asked him if he had time to talk. He told her that for her, he had all day, and with that, they talked for at least two hours until Carmen, fearing someone would come, reluctantly told him she had to go. Before hanging up however she told him she would try to call him the next day. He asked for her number so that he could call her, and she said that it would probably be better for her to call. He didn't make much of it and said that was fine and said as long as he could talk to her, it didn't matter to him who called.

After that first call, they were inseparable. They spent each moment they were free during and after school together. She called him every day and he would even go by her house after school while no-one was home and they would hang out in her room until she chased him off fearing someone would come. There were many close calls when her family, especially her brothers would come home unexpectedly while Corey was there, and he would have to jump out of the window to avoid running into them. Not that he was afraid of them or anything; Corey was a pretty tough guy and could hold his own with anyone. He just didn't want to make trouble for her, so he went along when she would ask him to sneak out of the window.

I am not really sure if her family knew about them seeing each other. We were pretty sure Sony, her middle brother did, and he had to. I am sure that Corey's family knew about Carmen because she spent lots of time over their house. They all loved her, and although Olivia didn't like that they were too young to be so close, she didn't make a big deal of it because Carmen was always such a nice and polite girl when she was around her.

The school year went by pretty quickly, and the following summer vacation Carmen and Corey spent most of their time with each other. She would pass by my house every day on the way to his house. Although they had been seeing each other pretty much every day for almost a year and had kissed and messed around, they had never done it. They were both only 16, Carmen was a virgin and Corey had very limited experience and after talking about it several times, they decided that the time had come to consummate their relationship. Summer was almost over, and if they were going to have time to do it, it would have to be before school started up again. So they devised what they thought was a fool proof plan. It was perfect, or so they thought. Carmen's dad always left for work at 9:00 a.m. and always worked late and didn't return until between 10:00 and 10:30 p.m. at night. Also, whether or not he got off early or got off at his regular time, he always called before he went home, to let whoever is there know he is on his way. So they would have plenty of time before he got home if he decided to not work a full day, but that was something he never did. Her mom would be leaving the house at around 10:00 a.m. that day to go and see a very sick friend, and she would be taking the bus to get there and then waiting for her dad to pick her up after he got out of work. Her brothers usually left he house at around 9:00 - 10:00 every morning during summer vacation to hang out with their friends and they would always plan it so they wouldn't return to the house until right before their dad go home.

The plan was for Carmen to call Corey at around 3:00 p.m. to let him know if the coast was clear. He would then walk to her house, she would let him in, and they would spend the rest of the day together until around 8 or 9 p.m., at which time he would leave before anyone got home. They would smoke a little weed to help them relax, and then they would do it. They would make love for the very first time, taking the final step to prove their everlasting and unending love and commitment for each other to be together forever. It was finally going to happen. It was a perfect plan. It was going to be the most beautiful and exciting experience of their young lives.

They were both filled with so many emotions that morning, afraid because of the danger that would be involved if anything were to go wrong with their plan and the excitement and uncontrollable and overwhelming desire to be together outweighed any fears that they had. Corey was really nervous as he left the house that afternoon after her call. He really wanted this to happen and he knew that they had planned it out so very carefully. There was a huge risk of them getting caught by doing it at her house, but there was something else that was bothering him. He'd never felt like he did about a girl the way that he felt about Carmen, and although he had been with a few girls before, this time would be different. He really cared about her and didn't want to hurt her in any way. It wasn't like before where it was purely for the curiosity and pure fun in doing it. He didn't really care much about the other girls. This time wouldn't be just having sex for the sake of the physical pleasure of it. With Carmen, he would actually make love to her, which was a whole new ballgame for him. This along with the slight thrill in the danger in doing it in her bedroom and in her house, made him very nervous, but at the same time was very exciting, and irresistibly enticing to him. While his mind was hesitant and telling him to be cautious, his body was telling him, let's do this.

As Corey walked up to Carmen's house he realized that there was no turning back at this point, but even if he could turn back, he wouldn't. This was something that they had planned and wanted to do for a long time now, and there was nothing that was going to stop them from going through with their plan. Carmen had been anxiously anticipating Corey's arrival. She constantly looked out of the window at the front of the house so she could see when he was walking up. As he walked up the walkway to the front door, she opened it before he had a chance to ring the bell. She took his hand, and quickly pulled him inside, and still tightly holding his hand led him to her bedroom and closed the door. He had been to her house before, but it had been late night when he'd snuck in her bedroom window when everyone was asleep. He'd never been there in the daytime or come through the front door however, and had never been there for the reason he was there for that day. Before it had been just to lay in her bed with her and to hold each other, whispering softly in each others' ears about the love that they felt, and about what their plans were for the future. This was a totally different situation however, and their plan to make it happen had worked perfectly up to this point. Both Carmen's parents and her brothers were not home and wouldn't be back for hours. They had the place to themselves. The moment that they had been waiting and dreaming about had finally arrived. There would be nothing and no-one that could stop them from doing it now, and they had every intention of making the moment as memorable and beautiful as they dreamed and hoped it would be.

The time had finally come for them to consummate their love for each other. As they entered her room and sat down on her bed, he could tell from the trembling of her hand that she was very nervous. This would be her very first time and he wanted to make sure that she was ok and that she would be able to enjoy herself. At first she was very quiet and hesitant, not really looking in his eyes when she talked. He asked her if she was sure she wanted to go through with their plan, and she told him that of course she was, but she was very nervous, not because she wasn't sure that she wanted to do it, but because she had never done it before. She said that she wasn't afraid of how it would feel while they were doing it, but she was afraid of how they would both feel afterwards. He comforted her, held her hand and looking into her eyes said:

"Everything will be ok."
"It will make us closer than we were and take us to another whole level of love that will form a bond that no-one can break, ever"

He then told her that he'd brought a joint for them to take a few hits of before they got started, just to take the edge off.
"I want us to really enjoy our first time together."

With that, he pulled the joint out, lit it, they both took a few hits off of it, and waited for it to take effect. He made sure that she only had a few small hits, because she had only smoked weed with him a few times before, and he didn't want the effects of the weed to make either one of them get too high and not allow them to enjoy the experience and closeness of what they were about to do. After a few minutes, he could tell that she had begun to relax and feel more comfortable. He took her hand and looking into her eyes again, he softly kissed her lips, and whispered in her ear:

"Are we ready?"

"Yes, we're ready," she replied, and they both got undressed, laid down, and slowly and gently did what they had planned to do, consummating the love that they had started just one year before. It was more beautiful and painful than she had thought, and it was just as he'd imagined it would be. They had finally gotten to go to their Tropical moonlit beach.

As they laid there they both drifted off into a light and blissful sleep, completely consumed with the euphoric and satisfying feeling that they had from what they'd just done, and completely oblivious to the sound of someone coming home and entering the house through the front door. Caesar had come home earlier than they'd planned, but with the door to Carmen's room closed, the music playing, and the lingering effects of the weed, they were oblivious to the fact that he had come home and was on his way down the hallway. As he walked down the hallway he smelled the faint aroma of the weed that they'd attempted to cover up by opening the windows to her room. As he approached her bedroom it seemed as though the smell was coming from there, so he angrily pounded on her door and asked if she was in there. Carmen and Corey were still lying across her bed partially dressed and half asleep and the violent and angry banging on the bedroom door startled both of them and woke them up. Caesar screamed,

"Carmen, why is your door locked and who is in there with you?"

There was no answer, so he pounded on the door again, and angrily yelled, "Carmen, open the door right now. If you don't open it I am going to break it open!"

The joyful bliss that the couple had been feeling quickly turned in to fear and panic. Their plan, which had worked perfectly up to now, was quickly unraveling. This was the last thing they ever figured would happen. Now everything had gone terribly wrong and Corey was trapped in the room with his only escape being the bedroom window that led to the front of the house. If he jumped out of the window, and the coast was clear for him and no-one saw him, he could get away and everything could still turn out ok. She could then tell her brother that no-one was in the room with her, and that the smell of drugs may have been coming from outside or something like that, but partly from fear and panic, and partly from the weed that had not yet fully worn off they panicked, and were not thinking clearly, and as the banging and her brother's voice getting louder at the door insisting that she open it or he would break it down, Carmen whispered

"Quick, hide in the closet and I will get rid of him."

Corey kissed and hugged her, and quickly hid in the closet, gently closing the door behind him. Carmen quickly straightened her bed, fixed her clothes and went to the door to open it. As she slowly opened her bedroom door her brother quickly pushed his way in almost knocking her off of her feet.

He yelled again, "Who is in here with you?"

Trying very hard to not show any fear, and to sound convincing enough that he would believe her, she said, in a slightly angry tone

"What are you talking about? No one is in here. Why are you tripping?"

He continued to yell, "You're lying, and you better tell me who was in here with you. I know someone was in here."

By this time Carmen was beside herself with fear, and again she told him that no-one was in the room. Caesar looked around the room, looked at the closet, and walked over to it. Carmen was beside herself. This was it. They were going to be busted. What were they going to do? As he reached the closet the phone started to ring. He looked at her as if he wanted her to answer it, but seeing that she wasn't moving, he ran out of the room and went to the kitchen to answer the phone.

After Caesar left the room, Carmen quickly closed her door, opened her closet to let Corey know the coast was clear, grabbed his hand and quickly led him to her window. It was just around 8:30 p.m. at that point and it had started to get a little dark. Corey kissed her on her forehead, told her he loved her and asked her to try to call him later. She said that she would try, told him she loved him, and helped him climb out of the window, and lay back down on her bed trying to pretend that she was sleep.

The series of events that took place from that point on that evening is unclear and differs depending on who you talk to, but whatever happened and however it happened, a few minutes after that, the sound of gunfire filled the air, Corey had been shot and was laying on the sidewalk in front of the Martinez house with two gunshot wounds to the chest. He'd been shot, and he was lying there on his back, with blood coming out of his mouth and chest.

When the police cars arrived to the scene, Caesar was kneeling over Corey with a gun in his hand, a .38 Special. As the policemen exited their vehicle, they drew their weapons, aimed them at Caesar and ordered him to drop the gun. He, perhaps still in shock, didn't drop the gun right away, looked up at them with a half dazed look on his face. They ordered him once again to drop his weapon. This time he did hear them and complied. The two officers immediately pounced on him with their knees in his back and with his face down in the grass. At this point a crowd had started to gather and one of the officers called for backup. Carmen came running out of the house and saw her brother handcuffed and face down in the grass with the officers both still with their knees in his back. As she began to ask what was going on and to ask what they were doing to her brother, she looked over and saw Corey, her love, her soul mate, lying motionless in a pool of blood. She screamed in agony.

"Oh my God, Cory!"

She bent over holding her stomach as if someone had punched her. She slumped to the ground and crawled over to Corey, first crying loudly and then sobbing. The crowd at the scene was beginning to grow, and not really knowing what was going on, began to become a little noisy and rowdy.

By this time someone had told Elijah and Olivia that something had happened to their son, and they both came running down the block to find out what happened. Elijah reached the scene first and was horrified to see his son lying there, motionless, almost looking like he was asleep. He screamed,

"Dear God, no. Not my boy!"

He turned to catch Olivia before she reached the scene. He tried to grab her and hold her back, but he couldn't. She shoved him aside and shoved her way past the officers also attempting to hold her back. As she forced her way past them, she kept saying

"That's my baby, that's my baby, that's my baby, I have to get him home, he needs to come home"

She was in shock. By this time Elijah's sorrow had quickly turned to anger, and he approaching the officers screaming at them, " What the fuck happened? Who shot my boy?"

The officers said they didn't know. He then looked over Caesar who was sitting in the back of one of the patrol cars at this point, and he rushed up to the car, screaming at Caesar, asking him if he killed his son. Caesar shook his head no, and softly kept repeating that he didn't do it. The officers, after talking amongst themselves for a few moments, decided the best thing to do would be to get Caesar away from the crime scene as quickly as possible for his safety, and prevent the possibility of the situation becoming ugly and out of control really quickly. So the car that Caesar had been put into took off, taking him down to headquarters for questioning. The remaining two cars stayed there and quickly dispersed the crowd that had gathered, talked to Elijah and Olivia, giving their condolences and telling them that everything would be done to find out what happened and to bring the perpetrator of the crime to justice as soon as possible. They then took them home and began asking them a few questions about Corey and basically just getting some preliminary information from them, nothing too in-depth at that time as they were both very upset, especially Olivia who was inconsolable at this point. They then went back to the Martinez house to question Carmen and her parents, Edgar and Lola, who had both arrived right after the police had taken Caesar away. They asked them a few questions about their relationship with the Jenkins, and their son's relationship with Corey. They said that they did not know them well, but that there had always been a cordial relationship, as they were neighbors and lived in the same neighborhood. They then asked Carmen if she knew Corey, but before she could answer, Edgar interrupted her and told the officers that they would not be answering any more questions until they had a chance to talk to an attorney. They officers said they understood. Edgar then asked what would be happening to his son, and the officer said they would be taking him downtown for questioning and that he would probably then be booked in the county jail. They said he would need to wait to be arraigned, and after that he would probably be charged with murder. Carmen was still in shock, and still confused as to what happened. At that time, believing that Caesar had committed the murder, she was completely enraged and angry at him and felt that he should pay for what he had done. He had taken her one true love and soul mate away from her.

Caesar would be tried, agree to a plea bargain, and do hard time for the next seven years at Folsom State Prison for involuntary manslaughter. For the Jenkins family, losing their youngest proved to be devastating and the family never really recovered to where they'd been before, a loving and close family. It seemed to splinter the family group as though Corey was the glue that had held them together, and once he was gone everyone seemed to go their separate ways including Pete. The loss of their son put a huge strain on Elijah and Olivia's relationship and after trying for two years after his death to hold it together, the strain finally proved too much for them and they divorced after 26 years of marriage. For the Martinez family, they too would lose a son for a long while, and their lives would also never be the same. They would be ostracized in the community, fair or not, and their entire family, not just Caesar, would be blamed and punished by the community for Corey's murder.

After Corey's death things got really bad between the Latinas and Blacks in the neighborhood for a while. Eventually however, the community began to slowly heal and everything began to settle back to normal. The days, weeks, months and years ahead however would never be the same for any of us. For the Jenkins, who'd lost a son and a brother, justice would be served, but the days would never be as bright or happy and the pain would never go away, and their hearts and lives could never again be the same. For Carmen, the loss of Corey was devastating. She would become hard and cold towards her family and towards people in general, building a huge protective wall around herself to protect her from feeling anything. She would go on to dedicate herself to her school work so that she could go to law school and realize her dream of being a lawyer. That would help her to block out the deep feelings of hurt that she knew would never go away no matter where she went, what she did, or who she ever became involved with. As for me, Ace, Q, Juju, and the rest of our friends, our lives would be changing from that point on. The murder of our young friend suddenly transformed us all from being young, wet behind the ears teens without a care in the world, no worries of things to come, living day to day and not worrying about tomorrow, into the world of young adults, dealing with the realities of life, responsibilities, falling in love, being hurt, paying bills, having kids, dealing with the deaths of loved ones and those who are close to us, and dealing with the realities of life as adults. It would be different from that point on. Life was no longer just today, it was tomorrow, and the future had come upon us in the blink of an eye.

WE MEET AGAIN

I arrived at the Touch an hour early. I wanted to scout the place out and to have a drink before Caesar got there. I hadn't been there in a long time but it hadn't changed much. It was so dark in there you would think it was closed if you didn't know better. It smelled like cigarettes, and the smooth sounds of classic old school music was playing on the jukebox which was located close to the front door. I stood in the doorway for a moment to try and let my eyes adjust to the darkly lit room, and then I proceeded to the end of the bar and ordered a drink, Hennessy straight up. I usually didn't drink Hennessy straight, but I needed something pretty strong that would calm me down before Caesar showed up. If I didn't, I would have probably lit him up as soon as he walked in the door.

Business at the Touch didn't look very good, or as least as good as it had been back when we used to go there. The bartender brought my drink, and after I paid and tipped him for it, my mind slowly started to drift again, trying to figure out why a man who I hadn't seen in seven years, a man who killed one of my closest friends and who knew I hated him with a passion, was so anxious to meet and talk with me. I just couldn't wrap my head around it.

As I was sitting there day dreaming I glanced up, and at the other end of the bar was one of the most beautiful women that I'd seen in a long, long time. She had beautiful skin, wavy hair, thick pink lips, which I love by the way, and she was wearing what looked like the tightest black mini skirt that she could find, which showed off her perfectly proportioned curbs and her flawless legs. As I stared in amazement at her, my gaze slowly made it down to what I consider one of the most important and sexy parts of a woman's body, her feet. She had on some of those high heel shoes they call candies, and I could see that she had perfectly manicured toenails on toes that were perfectly aligned and straight. She also had a toe ring on both of the second toes of both feet. You know the one next to the big toe, as Morris Day would say, so sexy. People think I am kind of weird because of my fetish for feet, and they are probably right, but in my eyes a woman with pretty feet is sexy, and there is nothing that is more of a turnoff than a woman with hammer toed feet. I am serious. I don't care how beautiful a woman is, if she has ugly feet, it totally turns me off. This woman's feet were perfect and I think she caught me staring at them because as I looked up she had a slight smile on her face. I didn't care if she saw me or not, but as a matter of fact, I hoped she did because at some point I intended to go over and holla at her and try to get her number.

I sat there trying to decide how I should approach her to find out her plans for the evening when suddenly my thoughts were interrupted as I felt a tap on my shoulder. It was Caesar. The fool actually showed up. I didn't think he would, and I was hoping that our conversation from the night before was actually a bad dream or something. But no, it wasn't a dream. Here he was, looking a little older of course, but for someone who'd been in prison for seven years, he didn't look that bad. He was what we called a pretty boy player back in high school, just like Q. He'd always had a sleek, muscular build, and always acted as cool as the other side of the pillow. He still had his good looks for the most part, but for someone who was only a few years older than me, he looked much older.

His voice cracked as he said what's up and reached to shake my hand. I just left him hanging. As I stood up and he went to hug me, I held my hands up and pushed him away. I knew that he had to have felt a great deal of guilt after doing what he'd done, and the main question I had for him was why? Why someone who we'd called a friend, who was from the block and one of us, killed a kid from the hood for dating his sister? It didn't make any since then, and it didn't make any sense now that we were standing there seven years later.

We sat down, he immediately ordered some drinks for us, and began trying to make small talk asking me how I was, and how my family was, and telling me about his life since he got out. When he talked his eyes looked as though he had a great pain in his heart and when he began to talk about his time in prison, his voice cracked. He told me about the ordeal that he and his family had gone through while he was locked up, and what they were going through since he'd gotten out. I didn't particularly care anything about what he was going through, but I did have pity for his family for having to endure what they'd been through because of him. As he spoke I just sat there listening to him, drinking my drink, waiting until he got to the point of why he called me there and what he had to tell me.

After taking a long pause and then a few deep breaths, he finally began telling me his version of what happened that day, and what he had to tell me would shake me to my core. He began by saying that he didn't shoot Corey, something that he had never said before, so when he said it, I basically told him that I didn't want to hear it and if that is what he asked me to come there to tell me, he was wasting both of our time.

He then proceeded to tell me what had happened the day that Corey was killed, taking me back to that night and describing in detail his version of the events that led up to his murder. He said he'd gotten home that day after hanging out and getting high with his friends. This was quite a shock to me at the time because we'd always though he was the straight laced one in the family.

He then continued:

"My parents didn't get home yet, and I thought Carmen was in her room asleep because her light was out. When I passed her room though, it smelled like someone was smoking weed in there, so I banged on the door to ask her who she had in there with her. I went to try to open it, but it was locked, so I banged on it and told her to unlock it and let me in. I walked in, and we started arguing about someone being in there with her, and that I smelled weed in her room, and then the phone rang. I went to answer it and it was my dad calling to tell me that they were on their way home. I told him ok, but I didn't tell him about what was going on with me and

Carmen because I didn't know for sure yet and I didn't want to cause any problems until I found out what was up.

"After that, I went back to her room but she looked like she was asleep, so I closed her door and went to my room to kick back until my parents came home. "

"When I got to my room, but before I could lay I heard a loud sound that sounded like a car backfiring, so I ran to my dad's room to get his .38 that he kept in the upper shelf of his bedroom closet, and I ran out the front door to see what caused the noise. "

"Once I got outside I saw Corey laying there in front of the house, and he wasn't moving. I ran over to him to see if he was ok, and I saw he'd been shot in the chest and shoulder and he was unconscious. "

Right after that everything got crazy. Two or three police cars pulled up, told me to drop my gun, took it from me, cuffed me, and sat me on the curb.

"I didn't really know what was going on, but I knew I didn't do anything wrong, and I knew I didn't shoot Corey"

He said that at that point all of the neighbors came flowing out of their homes to see what was going on and then Carmen came running out of the house. And upon seeing him standing there with the gun in his hand and Corey lying in front of him in a pool of blood, she screamed a blood curdling scream, "Caesar, what did you do? You killed him, you killed him. What did you do? "

He said that she ran over, picked Corey's head up and laid it on her lap, and leaned over him sobbing uncontrollably. He said that after that everything just started happening so quickly that it is all kind of a blur. He does remember Corey's parents arriving on the scene, seeing all of the neighbors. He said that after hearing what Carmen said, it quickly began turning into a mob scene, and the police called for backup in anticipation of there being trouble.

He said that he heard the police call for two more cars, and that one of those cars came flying around the corner within a few minutes of being called. The officers from the second car quickly began dispersing the mob that had been gathering around the scene, moved him into the backseat of their car and took him off to jail. Once at the jailhouse, he said that he was thrown in a cell for a few hours before being taken to a room to be questioned about what happened. He said that it was in that room where his fate was sealed.

He then said that there were two officers in the room, one black and one white, and they begin grilling him with questions about what he knew and saw in regards to the shooting. He said they grilled him for hours, never telling him his rights, continuously telling him that he was not a suspect and that they were just trying to get as much information and help from him as possible so that they could solve the case as quickly as possible. He said that it was after 3 to 4 hours of the questioning that he slowly realized that the tone of the interview began to turn, and the questions started to become more like accusations and them telling him what happened instead of him telling them. He said that after 5 hours of this questioning he was so tired and hungry, but the offices kept promising him that they were almost finished with him and that he would soon be able to go home to his family.

His parents contacted a family friend who was a lawyer who raced down to the precinct to post bail for him, and to notify the police that he would not be answering any more questions that they had for him. He said that by that time it was too late, and that after hours upon hours of sitting in that small room, answering question after question, being tired and hungry, and being constantly told he would be going home, he broke, and the officers finally got him to confess to what they wanted to hear. That he'd shot Corey thinking he was an intruder, and thinking both he and his sister were in danger. Saying that he came home, heard what he thought was a prowler outside of his sister's window, got his father's gun, went outside to confront the intruder, and then seeing him in front of the house shot him, and that it was only then that he saw that it was Corey. He said that at that point they had a full confession of guilt, and even though they had never read him his rights, they said that because he was not a suspect and hadn't been arrested, that they didn't need to read him his rights, and that everything that he said had been voluntarily given by him. He then said that by the time the trial came, not only did they have the evidence and his confession to convict him; they didn't have any other suspects because they never tried to find one. If the case went to jury he was looking at doing at least 20 years.

He then said they offered him 7 years for manslaughter as an alternative to serving 20 to life if convicted of 1st degree murder, which his attorney convinced him they had a very strong case for. He said that then, as a result of the recommendation of the terrible lawyer he had, he reluctantly agreed to plead guilty. He said he was so young, confused and scared at the time, he felt that he didn't have a choice.

I was totally blown away by what he was telling me, and my anger and frustration quickly turned into confusion and sympathy because the crazy thing was, I started to kind of believe him. The only thing was, if he didn't do it, then who did? Who, after seven years, got away with the murder of my friend, and put Caesar, his family, and all of us through the nightmare that we have gone through over the past seven years?

Caesar then continued.

"One day, not long before I got out, I felt really sick and I went up to a CO to tell him that I needed to go to the infirmary. He told me to get out of his face, and that I wasn't going anywhere but back to my cell. I told him that if he didn't take me to the infirmary I would report him, and he looked at me, kind of smiled, and said, you don't remember me do you? I told him I didn't and he said that's ok; ask your boy Corey if he remembers me.

The guard went on, "Oh, that's right, Corey ain't around any more, we took care of that piece of shit and sent you up here to pay for it."

He said that after that, the CO told him to get the fuck out of his face and to get back to his cell.

"I couldn't believe what I was hearing and I wanted to drop him right in his tracks, but I was so close to getting out I didn't want to mess myself up. All I could do was stand there."

After that, the CO told him to stop crying like a little bitch and to keep his mouth shut or he and his buddies on the outside would kill him, or his family in front of him, and then kill him.

My mouth dropped open when those words came out of his mouth. It was partly in shock, partly in disbelief, and partly in anger. I didn't know what to say and I didn't know if I believed him. How is this man going to sit up here and tell me that he didn't kill Corey when all of the evidence in the case said he did it without a doubt? That, plus the fact that he did a plea bargain with the DA for a lesser charge of aggravated manslaughter, which is why he only did seven years. I told him he had to be fucking kidding me. I asked him how he could sit there and look me straight in the eye and tell me he didn't kill my boy and that someone else did. He took another deep breath and said because it is true, and that I had to believe him because I was his last hope. He said he was running out of time and that he wanted to finally get the truth out in case something were to happen to him. He said that since Cory's death, and especially since he'd been out, he and his family had been treated like garbage by the community, and there had been many threats on their lives, especially recently. I still didn't have very much sympathy for him, but his claim automatically raised my interest as to what he would say next. He said that after he heard I was doing some work as a private investigator and I was so close to what happened he felt that this would be a good time to try and unburden himself with what had been weighing on his mind for all these years. He said that he wanted to tell me because he knew I could help him prove what really happened that day.

Seeing that I possibly believed him, Caesar paused for a moment, and as he began to speak again we heard an argument breaking out on the other side of the bar. As I looked up I could see that it was the woman who I'd been admiring earlier in the evening arguing with some white guy who, by what I could hear from the conversation, she probably knew. He was drunk, and accusing her of flirting with me, and as they argued, he slapped her in the face and pushed her into Caesar. She then fell to the floor. I helped her up and asked if she was ok. If there is one thing that I can't stand it is when a man puts his hands on a woman, any woman, and at that point I was hoping that he would say something so that I could show him just how much I didn't like it. He grabbed my arm and screamed at me to keep my hands off of her. I snatched my arm away from him, and just as I was about to swing, I saw a fist go by my face, striking the guy square in the jaw. He flew back, about 10 feet at least, and landed on the floor under one of the tables. He was out for the count. It was Caesar who'd laid him out with one punch. I could see he'd hit him so hard that blood from either his nose or mouth had landed on the bar and the change that I had laying there. I picked it up, leaving the money with the blood on it for a tip, and told Caesar we had to get out of there. Before we left though, I asked the girl again if she was ok, and apologized for what happened. She thanked me for what we did and that there was no need to apologize because the guy was an asshole. She then paused for a moment, took my hand and said that he had actually been right, she was flirting, and then she placed a paper with her number on it in my hand and said her name was Hope and to call her sometime. I said I would of course, and we ran out of the door. Once outside and down the street we decided that it would be best to split up at that point and both go our separate ways, but before parting ways we made plans to meet the next day to discuss the rest of what he had to tell me. I told him that we should stay out of that place for a while after what happened until things cooled off, and he agreed. At least he told me he did. Little did I know that he had no intention of not going back for a while, and as a matter of fact, he planned on going back in after I left him. He had always been like that. Stubborn and fearless to a fault, never seeming to think ahead of the consequences for his actions, or thinking ahead of things that may happen because of them. He felt that once he did what he did, and knocked the guy out, it was over. But little did he know how wrong he was. It wasn't over at all, not by a long shot.

As I drove home that night my mind continued to race with thoughts of what Caesar told me. Could we all have been wrong all of this time? How could we have been, it didn't make sense. How could such an open and shut, slam dunk case be wrong, and the wrong person have gone to prison for murder while the actual murderer was still out among us, perhaps closer than we could imagine. As I arrived home and went to bed, I laid there and continued to think, if it wasn't Caesar then who could it have been? Perhaps Caesar really knew and he was just about to tell me before we were interrupted, or perhaps he had an idea or some information on who it was, and that is what he was going to tell me. Either way, we'd made plans to meet at his hotel room the next day at 2:00 p.m., and he would tell me whatever was left for him to tell. Until then I would just have to wait.

When I woke up the next morning I immediately began thinking about what happened the night before. I wasn't going to be able to concentrate on work that day in anticipation of talking to Caesar later on in the day and finding out what he had to tell me. I made some coffee and went into my living room to drink it while I watched the morning news. As soon as I turned on the TV an immediate chill went throughout my body as I saw a picture of Caesar with the caption Breaking News Report scrolling below it. I quickly turned the TV up so that I could hear what was being said and the newscaster was reporting that he'd been stabbed to death, and from what he was saying it happened somewhere close to the halfway house that he'd been staying in, and that it looked like after he was attacked he tried to make it back there only to collapse on the front lawn of the halfway house. The newscaster identified him as Caesar Martinez and said that he'd just gotten out of prison earlier in the month after serving time for murder. He the said that the details were unclear as to what happened or what the motive was, but that preliminary reports were that he'd been in an altercation in a bar not too long before he was found. This couldn't be happening. I thought we'd both decided that we would leave right after we talked. I thought he would be going straight home but apparently he didn't. Was this a coincidence or could this be related to what Caesar had to tell me?

As I left the house for work that day my mind was spinning. I was tripping over the fact that I'd just seen and talked to Caesar the night before he was killed. I was also thinking about everything that he'd told me, and most importantly, what he'd started to tell me but was unable to. If what he told me was true, then everything that I thought up to this point about

Corey's murder was wrong. I had to do something to find out for myself what really happened? Who was actually responsible for my friend's death, and if it was somehow related to Caesar's murder? It would stand to reason that whoever killed Corey was also responsible for Caesar's murder, or was it just a coincidence?

Who could the killer or killers be? Could it have something to do with the story that Caesar had told me the night before? Maybe he was telling me the truth. Or, could it have been the guys from the North side that we'd played the night that Corey was killed? They had seen Corey with us at the mall, they were pretty hot when they left, and they did promise to get back at us. They wouldn't kill him over a basketball game though, would they? Could they have been trying to get revenge on us for being embarrassed in front of their girls? It seemed pretty far fetched, and if they were involved wouldn't the police have questioned them and found out what they did way back then? I needed to find out but I really didn't know where to begin. I did know that I had to come up with a step by step plan to find what I was looking for, and I figured the first thing to do would be to get some help. Not really knowing who was involved however, I had to be careful not to involve someone who might have something to hide or who might have been in on one or both of the murders. I was going to need to get help from people who I could trust and who possessed the special skills that would be required. It would also need to be people who would want to find out the truth just as much or more than I did. I needed a crew.

THE CREW

If I was going to be able to solve the mystery behind the murders of Corey and Caesar, the first thing I needed to do was get a crew of people that I could trust, and who I thought would be able to help me do everything that I needed to do in my investigation. The first person of course would be my ride or die partner in crime, Q. Although his life had become a continuous jump back and forth between that of the secular world, and that of being a player extraordinaire, his connections and access to people who might know things was much deeper than mine at the time. Plus, we had worked together on most of the other cases that I have solved in the past, and although he tended to get sidetracked at times either chasing women or chasing salvation, he was just as close to Corey as I was, and was just as determined and passionate about finding the killer or killers.

I also would get my cop friend James Cool to help. I'd met James a few years back while playing basketball in pickup games at Land Park. We just started talking about sports and what not, and it turned out that we both were Pittsburgh Steelers fans and knew some of the same people. He recruited me to play on a recreational basketball team, and after a while we became friends. I liked him because even though he was a white boy and a cop, he seemed comfortable being around blacks, probably because he grew up in the inner city and went to a predominantly black school in Memphis Tennessee. His parents were divorced and he said he lived with his mother in Tennessee until he was around twelve, at which point he started having a few problems in school. Both his parents felt it would be better for him to live with his dad here in Sacramento, because they felt he was at the point in his life where he needed a man's influence. His father was also a police officer. He was killed while on duty right before he retired. James said he became a police officer because he wanted to honor his father and follow in his footsteps. We became really good friends and have been ever since. He was a great deal of help in me getting all of the firearms that I have, and in helping me improve my shot to a point where I have actually won several shooting competitions.

The third person that I wanted to get was one of our OG partners from the park named Melvin Big Boy Patterson. He was an older guy that we knew who grew up in the Park in the 60s, and had been everything from a Black Panther to a member of the Fruits of Islam. He had his hand in everything going on in the park at one time or another, and his knowledge and contacts would be very valuable to us even though he was extremely paranoid, and would probably have a huge problem working with James. He had also helped me before on a few cases.

The most difficult person that I would need to recruit for my team would be Carmen, Corey's girlfriend and Caesar's sister. This would be difficult for two reasons, one because her brother had just been murdered, and two, she was too close to both of the murder victims and may not be able to think clearly, stay focused and keep an open mind. Her input could be key however because she worked in an office where she had access to lots of records we might need. She also had first hand knowledge of Cory's murder and may have talked to her brother Caesar prior to his death. She may know what he was going to tell me before he died.

Getting in touch with Q and Jimmy and getting them to help would be easy because I saw and hung out with them all of the time. Carmen would be a much tougher person to get in contact with, because I hadn't seen or talked to her since Cory's murder, which was almost seven years to the day. We also hadn't parted ways on such good terms and I would probably be the last person she would want to talk to, especially since her brother had just been killed. I needed to really finesse that situation in order to get her help. I would have to convince her somehow that I believed what her brother was telling me before he was killed, that I was trying to help her and her family find out what actually happened to him and who was actually responsible for killing Corey, which is of course what I was really trying to do.

That was all of the people I needed. Oh, I mean it was almost all of the people I needed. There was one more person that I was thinking of getting to help me, Willie Boy. His name is William Green III, or, as he is more affectionately known by those who know him, Willie Boy. Willie Boy was a very good friend of ours, but his help is the kind of help you don't really want to get or need. It is the kind of help that comes in handy however, in sticky situations where his skills and expertise are invaluable and can save your life. It sounds a little confusing and it is really complicated to explain, but the best way that I can describe it, is to explain the type of person Willie Boy is. To explain it the way it was told to me by this old Italian man that lived on our street when we were younger. This guy, who I am pretty sure was Italian, was someone who everyone in the neighborhood knew to have been involved with the mob when he was younger. He had gotten out of that life at some point, probably against his will, and moved to Oak Park several years before.

He used to sit out on his front porch and we would always go over to his house to help him mow his lawn and to pick up garbage and stuff like that, and he would always give us all money to go and buy candy at Tom's or Herman's market around the corner. After we were finished doing whatever it was we did for him on any given day, he would always tell us these crazy stories about when he was in the mob, but he would always tell them like he was talking about someone else. We all knew he was talking about himself, but we played along

One day after telling us one of his stories, he told us something that I will never forget to this day. As he saw Willie Boy, who was around 16 at the time, walking by, he said,

"You know, there are only three types of gangsters in the world. The first was a wannabe tough guy who became a gangster because he was really afraid, couldn't be tough on his own and needed lots of people and support around him to be tough. This type of gangster could be anyone, from any background, and they usually became gangsters by choice, and could have been something else, but chose the lifestyle.

The second type of gangster is a guy who was probably a nice kid when he was little, but because of the circumstances of his life, whether it be his home life, whatever, he turned bad at some point and started living the life. They were usually really tough guys, but they do have a point that they won't go past, and a line that they won't cross."

He then looked across the street at Willie Boy as he passed by and said,

"The third type of gangster is the type that is the most dangerous. They are born bad, are bad, and can never be anything else but bad. This is this type of gangster that no-one should ever mess or fool around with, trust, or try to befriend, because these types of people are psychopaths, who have no feeling, and cannot be friends with anyone. They are dangerous because you never know what will set them off, or, once they are set off, how and when they will stop. They are the monsters that we think about when we are awake and dream about when we are asleep, not because of anything that happened to them in their lives, but because they were born that way."

The whole time that he was telling us this he was staring at Willie Boy as he was walking past, and once he finished, he pointed at him and said,

"This kid here is that third type of gangster."

He then warned us all to either stay close to him or to stay away from him. We all pretty much already knew this about Willie Boy because we grew up with him and had seen him go to that other side, but since we grew up with him, and he had always seemed to like us, we figured it would be safer for us to stay close to him, and we have.

Two months had gone by since Caesar's murder and I'd already started doing a little investigating on my own, keeping my eyes and ears open, waiting to see how the police investigation into his death was going, and trying to see if I could hear any news from the streets on what actually happened. The thing was, since I'd moved away from the park I hadn't really been in the streets over there for quite a while, and when you haven't been out there and no-one really knows or remembers who you are, people don't trust you and it's hard to get anyone to tell you anything. Caesar's funeral had been the week before and I'd planned to go, but I changed my mind at the last minute. I guess I wasn't ready to face Carmen yet. I probably should have gone because as it was, I really didn't know how to get in contact with her, but the last time I'd spoken to her was years ago, and our interaction wasn't on very good terms. I tried the number that I had for her, but it had been disconnected.

It was Sunday morning and I got dressed and went to church. I hadn't gone in a while, but I felt that I really needed to go that day. It was a beautiful Sunday morning, and the service was great. The preacher's message that day was about finding one's purpose and the path in life that God has set out before us. He said that God set us all on a path in life from the time that we were born, and that there would be times that we would stray from that path, be fooled, and wander off on a different path thinking that the alternate road is a path that we should be taking instead, but we would soon realize that we are wrong, and it is only through God, and his son Jesus Christ, that we would be able to get back to the path that we should be on, and that it is only on that path that we would find our true purpose and truly be happy both inside and out. It was a beautiful message, and it was fortuitous that I came and heard him speak those words that day because it fit right into where I'd gone and where I currently was in my life. It was like I was meant to be there that day to hear what he had to say.

As I left the church I saw Ayesha Richardson, someone who had also grown up on 33rd and was one of Carmen's close friends when we were growing up. She was standing by a car talking to some people who had just left the church. I guess she'd also been at the church service. When I saw her I figured it would be as good a time as any to ask her if she had seen or could get me in contact with Carmen. Ayesha was always a very pretty girl and over the past seven years she had grown into a beautiful woman. We had a little thing going once upon a time back in the day. It was right after high school, but it was basically just a long one night stand for both of us, and it ended just about the time she went away to the service, to grow and to see the world, as she said. I lost contact with her after I got married and meant to call her after my divorce but I never did. I was told a few years back by someone that she met a guy named Arthur, got married, had a son, and then got divorced and moved back in with her mom on 33rd.

After she finished talking and started to walk towards her car, I walked up behind her and tapped her on the shoulder. As she turned around and saw who I was, I said hello, and asked her how she'd been. She smiled and seemed surprised to see me. She said hello, hugged me and asked how I'd been. I told her I'd been doing fine, and we stood and talked for at least fifteen to twenty minutes getting caught up on things and people that we both knew. I eventually asked her if she still kept in contact with Carmen, and her smile was replaced for a moment by a look of disappointment, as if she thought or assumed that the whole reason I stopped and talked to her was to find out how to get in contact with Carmen. She said yes, she still kept in contact but that Carmen had told her not to give out her number to anyone without checking with her first. I said it was very important that I contact her, and that it was pertaining to her brother and something that he'd told me the night he had been killed.

I then told her again how nice it was to see her, asked her if she gave out her number and if she minded if I could have it. The smile came back on her face as she reached into her car and took out a piece of paper and a pen, wrote both her and Carmen's numbers down and handed it to me. I told her I would call her soon, and she looked at me as if she didn't really believe me. She said she hoped I would, said it was nice seeing me, to take care, and to say hello to Carmen if I got in contact with her. I told her it was great seeing her too, that I would be calling her, and that I would tell Carmen hello when and if I saw her. As she drove off I kind of felt good about the fact that it was Sunday and I had at least told her the truth about two of the things that I'd said to her as she was leaving. Two out of three isn't bad.

When I walked in the door from church I immediately called the number that Ayesha had given to me for Carmen. Unfortunately I got an answering machine, so I left a message for her telling her that I needed to talk to her and that it was pertaining to her brother and what he'd told me the night he was killed. I left my number and told her to please call me back so we could make plans to get together somewhere to talk. I also told her to come by my office if she would be more comfortable doing that. Right after I left the message and hung up the phone, it rang. I quickly answered it thinking it was her, but it wasn't, it was James. He asked where I'd been and said he'd been trying to call me for over an hour. I told him that I'd been at church and that I'd found a way to get in touch with Carmen, and had left her a message to contact me. He said he thought I might be wasting my time with that and that he didn't think she would be much help, but that it may not be a total waste of time, as if to insinuate that I might have another reason for wanting to meet with her. I set him straight, and asked him if he'd been able to set up that meeting with the two officers from the night Corey was killed. He said that was why he had been trying to call.

He said that one of the officers was no longer on the force and had moved to the east coast not long after Corey's death, for family related reasons. He also said that he was able to track down the other officer at a cop bar called The Pine Cove, where he knew he hung out. He said that the guy was already pretty drunk when he found him, so he sat next to him at the bar, struck up a conversation, and asked him if he would be willing to talk to me with regards to the case and what happened that night. The guy said he wouldn't, so James asked the guy if he remembered anything about that night, or if he remembered if anything seemed different or strange about how the case went. The cop said he did remember the case, but that he couldn't really remember everything that happened exactly as it happened since it had been seven years ago. He continued, saying that he remembered that he and his partner arrived to find a guy with a gun in his hand on his knees next to what seemed like the lifeless body of another person. He then said:

"Once we exited the patrol car, we drew our weapons and aimed them at guy with the gun, and I ordered him to drop his weapon."

He said that at first the guy seemed like he didn't hear him or that he was ignoring him or something, so he screamed again to drop his weapon and to put his hands over his head.

He said the guy then looked at them and dropped the gun.

The guy then complied with their order to put his hands over his head, they laid him down on his stomach, put his hands behind his back, and cuffed him. At that point a young lady came running out of the house and began going crazy when she saw the victim laying there, and she started screaming at the guy who they'd handcuffed asking him why he did it. He said they then lifted him to his feet and took him back over by their patrol car. They asked him what happened, and what he'd done, and he told them that he came out after hearing gunfire and saw a car taking off, and found Corey laying there. He said they then asked him if he knew the guy who'd been shot, and he said that his name was Corey and that it was a kid from the neighborhood. He said at that point things started getting a little crazy.

"All the neighbors began to gather round and the guy's sister came running out of the house screaming at him and asking him why he killed the victim and that he didn't have to kill him."

Once the crowd heard her screaming they started getting somewhat hostile, and once the victim's parents arrived it really started getting out of control, so they decided to call for backup, which he said came a few minutes later.

At that point James said that he could verify that what the guy was saying was the truth, because he was in one of the cars that were called in to assist. I was a little surprised by this, because James had never shared that with me. He said the officer then said that once backup arrived on the scene they quickly attempted to disperse the crowd which was getting louder and unruly by this time. He told James that was pretty much all he remembered, but that James should know more about what happened after that because he was the one that took the guy downtown. I then asked James why he hadn't told me this before and he said that he really didn't think it was very important, because all he did was transport Caesar to the station. He then said that the officer remarked that as far as he was concerned it was a dead issue, and that the right person had been put away for the murder.

James said that he tried to get as much information as he could from the officer, but by that time the officer had gotten too drunk for him to be able to understand what he was saying, so he decided to leave it at that and try to get in contact with him again when he was in a more coherent state of mind. I told James thanks for trying, that I knew it was risky for him to do what he did, and that I really appreciated it. In my mind however I was thinking that I wish he'd been able to get the officer to meet and talk with me, because I would be able to get a better read on him and whether he was being honest and truthful in what he was saying, or, if he was lying or attempting to hide something. At that point I felt that it was what it was and that I just had to be satisfied with the information that James had given me. It bothered me that after knowing James for all of this time, and hanging out with him, and having talked to him on many occasions about Corey and his death, he'd never mentioned that he had been the officer that had transported Caesar to the police station on the night Corey was killed. That was a little odd, and it didn't really sit right in my mind. I kind of brushed it off at the time thinking even if he hadn't told me before, he was telling me now, but either way, I didn't think it was a big deal.

STICKY SITUATION

It was finally Friday and my day was almost over. I only had one more session to go for the day and I could go home. It was going to be a pretty short session because it was a client that I had already had several sessions with, and now he wanted to include his wife in our discussions. So all I was going to do that day was to meet with him and his wife, go over a few ground rules with them on our future sessions, and that would be it for the day, nice, short, and sweet. The client's name was Marcus (Buster) Wiley and he stood around 6 foot 4 inches tall and was built like a brick shit house. He was an up-and-coming heavyweight fighter at the time with a very impressive record of 20 wins no defeats and 20 knockouts.

In my sessions with him prior to that day he'd confided in me that he had a strong suspicion that his wife was seeing other men and had been for quite a while. When I'd asked him why he felt so strongly that she had been seeing other men, he said that even though he didn't have proof of her infidelity, she had changed the way she acted towards him over the last several months, she had become cold and less affectionate, and she was always getting all dressed up and going to happy hour or dinner with her friends and not coming home until late in the evening. I told him lots of women do that, but that it didn't mean that she was stepping out on him, and asked him if he had any other proof. He said that he didn't have any actual proof, and that there were times when he followed her and she was actually at the place she said she was going.

He still said however that he felt deep down inside that she was being unfaithful to him, and that I could help him find out whether or not she was lying to him. I explained to him that my job was not to expose whether or not people are lying to each other but to help them work out problems that they are having with their relationships, so that they can move past them and create a better life together.

I asked him, if he were to discover that his wife was seeing somebody else, or had been seeing other people, what he would do. Would he try to work on their relationship, attempt to discover what the sources of their problems were, and come up with some solutions that would help them in their relationship, or if it would be too much for him to handle. He said if he found out she was seeing other men he didn't know what he would do and probably wouldn't know until he found out. He said he didn't know if he could forgive her and try to move on with their relationship, or if he would snap, lose control of himself and do great bodily harm to her and to any man he found out she had been seeing.

In other words, he was very vulnerable at this point, so in our last session I told him that I would like to meet with both him and his wife for a session to find out if I might be able to hash out these trust issues that he seemed to have been having, in hopes that it would help them with their relationship. Today, however, I would just be meeting his wife, getting some general information from them about their issues, and setting up some future sessions for them if they wanted that.

Buster arrived at my office at around 3:30 p.m., but as he walked in I noticed that his wife was not with him. When I asked him where she was he said that she had forgotten something in the car and that she would be there shortly. As we sat down he said he really appreciated me meeting with them and helping him find out if his wife was lying about seeing other men. I again reminded him that even though it is true that I am able to do that, it was my policy not to do it, and that my goal was to help couples move forward from anything that has happened in the past. I told him that the only way I would be able to help him with the issue of infidelity would be if either he or she were to admit while meeting with me that they had been unfaithful. It would be at that point that I would be able to work with that issue and try to help them move on from that if possible. He seemed so desperate to know this however, so I told him I would do the best I could to let him know if I thought that she was. At that point his wife walked in the door, and it was there that things took a very ugly turn for the worst, and my Friday would not be ending as quickly and as smoothly as I thought. It was the woman who I'd met the night that Caesar was killed. I'd been seeing her casually for the past few months, and up to this point I thought she was free and clear of any relationships or complications, which is why I had been seeing her in the first place. When I first met her she introduced herself as Hope, and after that night I called her and we'd hooked up several times and she never gave any sign or indication that she was married or even involved with anyone. But here she was now, standing in my office next to her husband who was going to be introducing me to her, and I had to not only act like this was my first time meeting her, I was supposedly going to read her and tell him whether I thought she was messing around on him.

He introduced her to me as his wife, Laura Wiley, and as I shook her hand it was trembling. Her voice cracked slightly as she said hello, and as I looked into her eyes, she had the look of a little girl who had just gotten caught by her father with her hands in the cookie jar. I shook her hand, said it was a pleasure to meet her, and asked her to have a seat. I was a little in shock, and I didn't know what was going to happen at this point. Would she remain calm and wait to see what I was going to say or do, or would she panic, break down and confess all of her sins, including her sins with me, right there in front of her husband, causing him to fly into a rage and to kill us both right there? I had to remain calm and cool, and do what I'd planned to do from the start. I could do this. I would continue to act like I'd never met her, pray that she would do the same, conduct the interview as I'd planned, hopefully come up with a quick plan for them to work out their issues, and hope that they would say that they would not need to come back for future sessions. Once the session was over, and he asked me what I saw when I tried to read her, I would say I didn't see anything in observing her that would indicate that she was seeing anyone else, and I would be telling the truth because she had me fooled for two months now thinking she was a single woman.

I began by asking her a few things about herself and when she answered them I had to act like I was hearing them for the first time, which I wasn't. I then went on to ask her questions about how she saw their relationship, how she felt about her husband and why, if she was happy, and if she had any issues with him or with their relationship. She began by saying that she loved her husband very much, and that they'd been married for two years at that point, and that their relationship was what she'd always dreamed it would be like when she got married. She then said that once his boxing career started to take off, she quit her job as a teacher, something that she loved, so she could travel around with him for his fights, and to be supportive for him and what he was trying to do with his career. She said that it worked for a while and that she was happy just being a housewife, but that after a while she became depressed and bored because she never went anywhere or did anything, and she missed teaching; since he was always gone for training she had become lonesome, bored, and it seemed like her life had become meaningless. She said that she'd started going to work out at the gym so that she could feel better about herself, and that she'd met some ladies there who she started to hang out and go places with. She said they would go out to happy hour, dinner, go to the movies, or just hang out at each others' houses, but that those women's husbands would always come home at night to be with them, and that hers wouldn't always do that because he was out of town training or for a fight, and that she was by herself and lonely most of the time in the evening. So she said from time to time, she would go out by herself in the evenings to bars sometimes, just to have a drink or two and to relax. She said that she knew it wasn't very ladylike to do, but that she was not doing anything wrong, and that after her drink, should would always go home. I felt that it was a good time to cut her off at that point for obvious reasons, and I asked Marcus to tell his wife what his concerns were and why he had them, what he felt about her concerns, and how he felt about her. Once he did these things I quickly made some suggestions about what I thought they could do to improve their relationship and the trust that they had between them, and I gave my standard speech saying that while it appeared as though they were on a path to improving their relationship, if they would like to schedule some additional sessions I would be glad to see them, all the time hoping and praying that they wouldn't. Before Laura could speak however, Marcus said that they would probably like to schedule a few more sessions with me to make sure they are on the right track. I said that would be fine, and to see my secretary on the way out to schedule something. They both stood up to leave, and as I shook Marcus's hand he mouthed that he would call me probably to ask about what I read as far as his wife was concerned. As he walked away and out of the door I shook Laura's hand and said it was very nice to meet her, and as she took my hand she said it was very nice to meet me too, and then quietly mouthed the words "thank you" as if to say thank you for not telling her husband the truth about us. She then turned to walk away but before she walked out of the door, she turned to me again and said she was looking forward to our future sessions, and winked her eye. Was she kidding me? She had to be kidding me. Did she think I was crazy, or maybe she was. I was not into married woman, especially not one married to a 6 foot 4, 250 pound boxer. If I had it my way, I would never see either of them again as long as I live. Hopefully they would go home, work on the things I told them to do, and never have to come back to me again.

After they left I was just finishing up some notes from the session and thinking about getting off work, going straight home to my nice, cool, air conditioned crib, cleaning myself up a little, maybe fixing me a nice stiff Myers and coke, throwing on some old-school jams, and maybe calling up a young lady to hang out, relax and kick back for a while, and maybe if I was lucky, getting a little something going on if you know what I mean.

Just as I finished up, locked my desk, and got up to leave, I was frozen in my tracks as I glanced up and saw her walking through my office door. It was Carmen, and to say that she was breathtakingly gorgeous would be a huge understatement of the facts. Looking at her literally took my breath away for a moment. She was beautiful in every sense of the word. She stood around 5"8 in her heels, which were very high to say the least. Her face was that of an angel and her body was that of a Hustler centerfold model. Her hair, which flowed just past her shoulders, was as black as coal and seemed to shimmer as the sunlight hit it from the window as she walked towards me. From her somewhat dainty but slightly muscular shoulders, her hourglass figure, down to her extra ordinarily flawless and slightly bowed legs and ending at her perfect feet, she was gorgeous. It had been around 7 years since I'd seen her, and she was even more beautiful than I remembered.

When I was finally able to gather my senses I asked her to have a seat, thanked her for coming, and told her how nice it was to see her. She responded saying how nice it was to see me too, and that it was a shame that the last rime we'd talked was so long ago. I'd gone to her brother's funeral but I went late on purpose so that I could stand in the back, pay my respects, and then sneak out without having to see or talk to her. I agreed, and apologized for that being the case, and said that we should not keep things that way. She looked at me with a very serious look on her face, and said, that's up to you. She then let a slight smile come across her face, but just a quickly as it had come, it went away.

We sat down and talked for a while getting caught up and reminiscing, and as we did my mind took me back to the old days growing up in the Park, Oak Park, 33rd Street, and the endless days of fun we all had there. Life was so simple then. Summers seemed longer, worries seemed to be here one day and gone the next. We all felt invisible, and immortal, not worrying about tomorrow and just enjoying the day. Man how things change as you get older. The older you get and the more responsibilities you have, the shorter the summers get, the less invisible and immortal you feel, the more you worry about tomorrow, and the faster time flies. We talked for at least an hour when I realized the time and even though it was great seeing her and talking about old times, I explained to her that I was just leaving the office when she came in. She apologized and I said there was no apology necessary but that I had planned to make a few stops on the way home and asked if I could stop by her place later in the week so that we could get caught up further, and so I that I could talk to her further about her brother and what he and we'd talked about the night before he was killed. She said that would be fine with her. I said that would be great, told her how nice it was to see her, and proceeded to turn off the light, leave the office, and to escort her to her car. As we got to the parking lot, she stopped next to a black Convertible BMW and said this is me, to which I said, wow, really, I guess your firm is paying you well these days huh? She smiled, hugged me and said, yes, very well, I see you have been keeping track of me, see you later this week. As she turned to walk to the driver side of the car, I couldn't help but notice how the dress she was wearing hugged her body and her ass perfectly, and when she got into the car, the split in the front of her skirt had nowhere to go but open, and the slightly setting sunlight hit her beautiful face and flawless legs perfectly. She started the car, waved goodbye, and disappeared from sight as she drove out of the parking lot. Suddenly, a strong sense of guilt and shame began to overcome me. What was I doing asking my dead friends girlfriend if I could go by her house. Even though it had been 7 years since anything other than a friendship, and to be there for her if she ever needed me. As I got in my car and headed home, my thoughts became calmer, and I began to rationalize and question what I was tripping over. I thought, that is what I am trying to do, help her and be there for her, just like Corey would want me to be. I was helping her, and when I go to her house it would be fine. I would tell her what I know, find out if she knows anything that would help, tell her what we planned to do to try to find out what actually happened to Corey, and if her brother was innocent of the crime and ask her if she would like to help. That was it. That was all I would be doing and there was nothing to feel any guilt or shame over. I would be fine.

TRIP TO THE NORTHSIDE

I asked Q and James to come by my house to shoot a little pool and to hang out for a while. Once there I explained to them what happened and what I was planning to do. After I finished telling them what Caesar told me, the first thing Q asked was if I believed what he said? I said no, I don't believe he is telling the truth, I know he is. That is all it took for him, he knew that I would never say I know something about anything unless I was absolutely sure or believed I was anyway. He knew about my gift for reading people because he'd seen me use it use it many times before, and I was always right. Getting him to agree to help me was easy. He had helped me several times in the past and he was very good at getting information that I needed but didn't have access to.

As far as James was concerned, I needed to explain to him that some of what we would be looking into may involve some of his fellow police officers and that we may find some things that may be difficult for him see or know. I told him that if he didn't feel comfortable doing this, that he should let me know now and probably not get involved. That way he wouldn't know what we were doing, and wouldn't be obligated to tell anyone anything. I also told him that if he wasn't going to help, that I would appreciate it if he didn't tell anyone what was going on. He said he would definitely like to help as much as he could without putting himself, his family or his job in jeopardy, but in either case, he would keep what we were doing a secret.

We decided that the best place to start would be way back at the beginning, the hoop game that we played against the Northsiders the day Corey was killed. It would probably be very difficult to find them after 7 years, but we might be able to track down one or two of them to ask them if the may have decided to cruise around the Park for a while before they left that day, looking to find someone to take their frustrations out on. They had threatened to get us back, so I wanted to have a conversation with them if we could find them to see if they may have been involved or what they might know. I remembered a few of the guys names from them being on their schools team during the time we played high school ball, so I would first see if I could find their names, phone numbers and or addresses in the phone book. If I did, I would try to contact them by phone to set up a day that I could meet with them to ask them questions about what they'd done after the game that day. If I didn't have any luck in finding them that way, we would have to jump in the car and take a ride over to the north side to drive around and see if we can find any of them that way. This would be a very tough and dangerous thing to do because the north side where these guys come from was always just as dangerous as Oak Park, especially for outsiders, and particularly for outsiders coming around asking questions. We would all need to be strapped of course, but at the same time, we would need to tread lightly so that we could possibly get the help we need from whoever we find. If we were going to go to the north side snooping around though, we would need some strong backup in case things got hot, someone who we trusted, and someone who could stand up to any amount of heat that we may find, someone like Willie Boy.

The next day was Saturday, and so I figured that would be as good a time as any to start. I told Q to pick up Willie Boy and then to come by and pick me up around 10:00 and we would head over to the north side to talk to Isaac Turner, one of the guys that we'd played that day. I'd been able to contact him on the phone and he agreed to meet us at the Robinson Center over off of Norwood in the heights. Isaac had played on Grants team back in the date try to run down some of the guys we'd played that day. I was able to contact one of them whose name was Isaac Turner. I spoke to him on the phone and he also remembered me from high school and from seeing me around town and out at the clubs over the past few years. He said he'd gone into the service after high school for two years, and upon his return he became a correctional officer. He said he would meet us over at the Robertson Community Center parking lot at around 10:30.

Q and Willie Boy arrived to pick me up the next day at around 10:30. They were in Q's cherry, midnight black, 1962 Lincoln Continental convertible with the suicide doors. It was sick, and he called it baby girl. It was pimped out with a red interior, original paint, and he'd just had a booming new Alpine stereo installed. I wasn't really into the whole low-rider thing, but Q was deep into it. So much so that he'd put four years into this car. I am more of a Mercedes or luxury car type of dude, but I guess to each his own. It was a beautiful car though. When they arrived I hopped in and we jumped on the freeway to take the 20 minute ride over to the North Side. While in the car, I made sure that everyone was carrying a little heat, and to tell Willie Boy to let me and Q do the talking once we got there to meet this dude. I had no idea what this guy could or would tell us or what his attitude would be, and were knew that Willie Boy tended to get a little impatient with people and could get heated very easily when discussing things with folks, especially when he didn't like what they were saying or if he felt that they were not giving him his due respect. I didn't tell him this, but I mainly wanted him with us for a little intimidation and as backup in case things didn't go smoothly. He was our enforcer and I have yet to see anyone who didn't fold under once he got going. the only bad thing however was once he does get going, it is very hard and even dangerous to try to intervene and get him to go the other way. That is why I felt it would be better if he just stood close by while we did the talking.

We arrived at the Robertson Center parking lot at around 11:00 and I could see that Isaac, the guy we were to meet, was already there waiting for us. He had his younger brother with him, a huge dude named Trevor that stood around 6'4 and must have been a bodybuilder or something because he had a bodybuilder tank top on and I could see that his arms looked to be around 18 inches around and his chest at least 50. Isaac pretty much looked the same. He also looked like he lifted weights at some point, but his belly stuck out farther than his chest. Q and I walked up to them and Willie Boy hung out by the car. Both Q and I had our hardware placed in the small of our back under our belt and covered up by our t shirts. So did Willie Boy. He actually carried two of them in case one wouldn't be enough. As we walked up to them we exchanged pleasantries and made small talk getting caught up on what we'd all been doing since we last saw each other. In reading them however I could tell after observing their mannerisms and the way that they were talking, that they really didn't want any trouble. They were not afraid by any means, we were in their hood, but they were not there to start anything or to cause problems. I asked him if he remembered what they did after the game that day and he said he that it was a long time ago and that things weren't that clear in his mind, but that since he'd talked to me he started remembering a little, and that he recalled that it was really hot that day, so after cruising around our neighborhood looking for someone to start trouble with, they finally calmed down, started getting hungry, and since they were running out of gas, they decided to head back home to the North side before it got too dark. I asked him if he happened to remember seeing our friend Corey after they left the park and I pulled out a picture of him and showed it to him. Again he said that it was so long ago that he really couldn't remember, but said he really doesn't think he remembered seeing him. At this point we began to realize that these guys had nothing to do with Corey's death so we shook their hands and they began walking to their car to take off. Before they left however I asked them if they were sure they didn't remember seeing the guy in the picture that night and I showed it to him again. I said he had walked up when we were beefing with them at the mall the day before. He then said that he did remember seeing Corey right before they took off for home, and that they saw him arguing with a white dude in front of a house. He said that he remembers his friend saying that he was one of the dudes that we'd argued with at the mall. It was then they decided to take off for the north side. I asked him around what time that was, and he said he remembered it being right around 8:30, when it starting getting dark.

Q and I walked back to the car and told Willie Boy what was up, and got in the car to take off. Just then, a car full of young want to be thug looking dudes drove up in a cherry red Lincoln that looked just like Q's except for the color and the suicide door. They were blasting their music and as they drove up the smell of chronic filled the air and I could see the smoke coming from their car. They parked right next to us. They were four deep and they were staring us down as soon as they drove up, and they didn't look like they were there to welcome us to their neighborhood if you know what I mean. They definitely looked like they could be trouble and could possibly looking to start some shit with us, but for their sake I really was hoping they were not. Unfortunately for them I don't think they realized that if they were looking to start trouble they picked the wrong people to do it with.

As the driver rolled down the window the smell of the weed got stronger as it came flowing out. After rolling down the window he loudly asked us what the fuck we were doing around there. Q and I knew that we had a ticking time bomb in the back seat, and if we said anything that would cause something to jump off, it would cause a chain of events that would send him down a road that we would like to avoid if possible. This was not the path that I'd plan on taking. I just wanted to go over there, talk to Isaac, and hopefully get some information from him that would be helpful to us. It was not working out that way however. These dudes didn't know it but they were in some serious danger, and although they looked pretty hard and might be dangerous themselves, they were putting themselves in the path of a monster from their most frightening nightmares, and we wouldn't be able to wake them up once things jumped off. I tried to tell them that we were just taking off but the driver quickly put their car in reverse and swerved it so it blocked us in our parking space. He jumped out of his car with a sawed off shotgun in his hand and started hitting the palm of his hand with it. He shouted,

"You mutha fuckas ain't going anywhere."

"We fixen to show ya'll what we do when we come up on punk ass Southside fools we don't like hanging out in our hood."

With that the other three fools jumped out of the car with their hands behind their backs as if they all were packing heat and were getting ready to draw on us. Q and I looked at each other as if we knew that even though we came prepared, they'd caught us off guard and it didn't look like this was going to go well for us. Q asked me what we should do and just when I started to answer that I didn't know, I heard a deep, calm voice from the back seat say,

"Turn the car off."

As we looked back at Willie Boy in the back seat, we could see that he was holding both his 9s in his lap. He looked Q in the eye and said,

"Turn the mutha fuckin car off and when I say now, both of ya'll duck down."

It didn't sound like a very good plan to me, but it was the only plan we had at the moment so I looked at Q and shook my head for him to go ahead and turn the car off. He did and we sat there as we heard the guys coming closer and telling us to get the fuck out the car. All of a sudden we heard Willie Boy say

"Now"

Q and I ducked, and I heard four bangs so loud it kind of stunned me for a moment. Both Q and I sat up with our guns drawn only to see Willie Boy facing the back of the car with his gun still pointed at one of the dudes with smoke coming out of it. He had the craziest look on his face, and he actually was smiling. He quickly turned to Q and told him

"Hurry up fool, let's go home."

Q quickly turned around, backed the car out smashing into the other car to make room, and took off for home. Willie Boy had shot all of them and they didn't even get a shot off. I was tripping but I was happy that Willie Boy had come with us because if he hadn't I don't know where me and Q would be right now. Actually yes I do, we'd be dead. We owed him our lives for what he did for us that day. The problem I had though was that what he'd just done didn't even faze him. Q and I were shaken up, and would be for a while.

When we got half way home Willie Boy told Q to stop by McDonalds for him to get something to eat. He said he hadn't eaten all day and he was hungry. We went by the drive thru at McDonalds on the way home. He ordered two Big Mac's and finished them off just before they dropped me off at my place. As they took off after dropping me, Willie Boy shouted to me to let him know if we needed any more help from him. It was like we'd just gotten back doing something enjoyable like bowling or playing hoops or something, not like he'd just shot four people and stopped for food on the way home. I told him for sure, but I was really hoping that I wouldn't need any more of his type of help. Deep down inside however, I felt that at some point in the not to distant future I would be calling him again.

As I sat in my living room that evening tripping off of what just happened, I started thinking about something that Isaac said when we were talking to him right before all the craziness broke loose. He mentioned that he'd seen Corey arguing with a white police officer at around 8:30 p.m., right before they took off for home. This seemed very odd because at that time of night on that block, it would be very unusual and damn near impossible for a white dude to be on that street, and why would he be arguing with Corey? Isaac had no reason or motive to lie however, so I had to assume he was telling the truth. Who was this white dude, and more importantly, why would Corey be arguing with him in front of Carmen's house at that time of night? I decided at that point that I would call James the next day to see if he could arrange for me to meet with the 2 officers who arrived on the scene first the night Corey was killed. I went to bed that evening still tripping off of what happened to us that evening, wondering what the repercussions would be the next day, and trying to think of answers to some of the questions that were that swirling around in my head.

When I woke up the next morning I made my coffee like I always did, but I hesitated turning on the news for fear of what I would see on what happened the night before. I was almost at the point where I just wanted to start skipping my morning ritual of coffee and news, and begin drinking my coffee on the way to work. I figured everything that I was seeing on the news at that time was bad news, so why should I be in such a hurry to hear it. My curiosity got the better of me though, so I finally figured I'd better turn it on, and as I did, I had a lump in my throat, and my heart began to beat at twice it's normal pace. As soon as I turned it on I saw a news report with the caption saying 4 men had been gunned down in Del Paso heights the night before. As I turned the volume up on the set, the newscaster was saying that the 4 men were gunned down by an unknown assailant, one was dead, two of them had life threatening injuries, and the fourth was in stable condition with non life threatening injuries. The report also said that when asked if he knew their assailants, the one that was in stable condition told them he couldn't recall anything about the incident, and the report went on to say that he was non cooperative when questioned further about the incident. I let out a huge sigh of relief as I realized that although someone had been killed and others had life threatening injuries, we'd dodged a bullet on this one. I went to church that day, I really needed it.

CARMEN

The next day was Monday and it was really warm. It was tough for me to keep my mind on work in anticipation of going to Carmen's house that night. Even though James didn't think she would be much help, I was really looking forward to talking to her in more depth about Corey and Caesar, and the night Corey was murdered. I had also never gotten a chance to talk with her since Caesar's trial and I had so many questions I never got answers to and that had been on my mind since then. I would finally be able to have her tell me what actually happened from her perspective. This was going to be intense, but I would try to make it as comfortable as I possibly could for her, for both of us.

There was actually also another reason that I was uncomfortable about seeing and talking to Carmen after all of this time, and why I had been avoiding her since Cory's funeral. It was something that I had never shared with anyone, including Q, and it was something that I feel a lot of shame and guilt over and I don't really know why. Maybe because Corey, although he was a couple of years younger than us was a very good friend of mine, and although what I did was really not that bad, because he died only a few days after it happened it really bothered me at the time, and it still bothers me to this day.

As I said before, Carmen was always a very pretty girl, and although she was one or two years younger than me, she always looked and acted a little bit older than she actually was. She was very pretty, innocent and sexy at the same time. She was shy and innocent, but also flirtatious especially with me. For some reason she always felt comfortable talking to me when she and Corey were together, and even when I would see her when he wasn't around. She would have to pass my house whenever she was on her way to his house, and sometimes she would stop and we would talk a few minutes before she would continue on. Nothing serious, just chit chat about how they were doing and how she was doing in school, stuff like that most of the time. As we got to know each other a little better however, she began asking me things about myself, like who I was seeing, or asking me stuff like, how many girls I was sleeping with or had I slept with or things like that. She would also look and talk to me sometimes in a way where I kind of felt that she had a small crush on me, even though I knew she was totally and fully in love with Corey. It seemed more like innocent infatuation more than anything else to me, and when I saw the conversation was going a little to far or getting out of hand I would always tell her that she'd better hurry up and get to Corey's house before he wondered where she was and get jealous.

One afternoon around a week before Corey was killed, I was outside washing my dad's car in my shorts with no shirt on. I always did that in the summertime when I was in front of the house washing cars or doing yard work, just in case some girls came by and I could show off the guns and abs. Anyway, I had just finished washing the car when I heard Carmen's voice say, "looking good", as she was walking up to me. I said, well it should look good, I just spent a lot of time cleaning it to make sure it looks good for pops so that he can give me my 50 cents for the job. She smiled and said, I wasn't talking about the car, and I said oh, and we both started laughing. I asked her if she was on her way to Corey's and she said no and that they were not speaking to each other. I asked why and she said that the day before they'd gotten into an argument about him flirting with other girls when she was around, and that they hadn't spoken since then. I then asked her where she was going, and she said that she came by to see me. I laughed again, a little more of an uncomfortable sounding laugh this time, and said oh, really, and why would you be coming to see me? She said, just to talk, and I responded that she'd better hope Corey doesn't see her here or she'd get in trouble, and that she knows he doesn't like her talking to me or anyone else for that matter. She said she knew and that he especially didn't like her talking to me. I asked her why, already kind of knowing the answer, but wanting to hear her say it anyway, and she said because he knows that she had a crush on me. She and I had always been very close, even when she started seeing Corey, too close as far as he was concerned. She had always been more like a little sister to me however, a little sister who was the girlfriend of one of my young homies from my hood. Corey was a kid that was a little younger than me who also lived on 33rd street back in the day. He was someone who I was very close to and considered more like a little brother than a friend.

At that point I felt that it would be better if I told her I was getting ready to go inside in hopes that that would cause her to leave, but when I told her I was finished with the car, and getting ready to head inside; she asked me who was home. I told her no-one was home right now but me, but that my brothers would be home from the park pretty soon. She then asked if she could come in until they got home. This caught me off guard, and after gathering my composure after actually considering taking her up on her proposition, and it was an unmistakable proposition, I laughed it off and said that it wouldn't be a good idea, and joked that I didn't trust myself and didn't want her to not like me anymore. She smiled and said I was crazy and that she could never not like me, and then after a few more seconds of uncomfortable silence, she said that she would come back another time, and I said ok. She then asked for a hug goodbye, something that she always did, but this time as I went to hug her, she kissed me on the cheek, and when I looked at her with what was probably a look of complete shock, she kissed me on the lips. Now comes the part that I feel guilty about. Instead of pulling away from her and immediately stopping what was going on, I did the exact opposite. I kissed her back. One of those long, slow, deep, French kisses too. It was the best kiss that I'd ever had and it lasted for a few minutes. Once we stopped I immediately felt a huge sense of embarrassment, guilt and shame all rolled into one. I apologized to her several times and told her to please not tell Corey what happened. At that point I believe she also felt guilt and shame even though she was the one who initiated what happened, and she said that she would never tell Corey and that it would be our secret. She then left and I went in the house and felt awful about what I'd done for the rest of the day. How could I have let that happen. How could I have betrayed my friend like that. Corey was killed a week later and after that, I completely broke off all contact with her, just to make sure nothing would happen. I mean I am human, and at the time I was a young man with hormones and things racing through my body, and she was a beauty. So I felt the best thing to do would be to cut off all contact with her at the time. She didn't understand why I was acting the way I was and thought that I was cutting her off and not wanting to be friends or be around her because I blamed her for what happened to Corey. She became very angry with me at the time and hasn't spoken to me since. She didn't realize though that while she was partly right about me not wanting to hang out or be around her, it wasn't because I blamed her for what happened to Corey, it was because I was afraid that I would not be able to control the feelings and desires that I had for her that I knew would come out if I were to continue to be around her, and out of respect to Corey, it was better for me to not be around her at all.

The day seemed really long and the time seemed to drag. I was getting a little more stressed about going to see Carmen and actually thought of changing things up and having her meet me somewhere else instead of going to her house. I didn't want to give her the wrong impression but I decided to keep the plan as it was. My goal was to find out two things from her, if she could remember anything or give me any information that might help me, and second, if she wanted to or thought she could help with my investigation. I was sure that it wouldn't be a problem for me, but I wasn't sure about her. I mean real talk, Corey was one of my home boys when I was younger and I would never do anything that I thought would disrespect him or his memory, but I was a 24 year old man at that time, and Carmen was a beautiful young women. Who knew what would happen when we were sitting there and the emotions and wine started to flow. I mean, I didn't anticipate anything happening, but you never really know. Anyway, I was a little nervous.

I told Carmen that I would be by her place at around 5:30 p.m. I headed home right after work to freshen up and then I went over to her place.

When I arrived at her house she answered the door in a silky, short robe and invited me to come in and to sit in the living room. She said she'd just gotten home and had just started to change when I rang the doorbell. I apologized and told her I would wait for her to change. She said ok, walked me to her living room and told me to have a seat and she would be right back. I could tell by the way that the robe clung to her body that she had nothing on underneath it, and no matter how hard I tried, I couldn't resist watching her as she left the room. When she returned she was wearing a long, colorful, tight fitting summer dress with a long split up the side. It was sleeveless, and I could tell she'd been keeping herself in shape because her arms and legs were toned, almost muscular, but still very feminine. She also wore sandals that showed off her feet.

This would be tougher than I'd thought. As she sat down on the couch next to me I apologized again for having gotten there a little early, which I actually hadn't. She said that she'd gotten off work a little late that day and had just gotten home and that she hoped I didn't mind waiting for her to change. I said of course not, hugged her, all the while telling myself to just concentrate on what I was there for. Deep in the back of my mind however, the mind of the young man of 24, I thought there is no way you can do this, so reschedule, make up some excuse, and you need to meet her another day. She asked if she could get me anything and I told her I could use a glass of water. She said how about a drink or something, and I said sure, how about a rum and coke. She said sure, but that she only had Myers rum if that would be ok. I said that would be great, thinking how could she know that my favorite rum was Myers? She couldn't, could she? She went to the kitchen to make my drink, and by the time she got back with a drink for both of us I'd finally composed myself and was able to concentrate on the reason that I had come to see her. I asked her how she'd been since the last time I'd seen her, how her mom and dad were doing, and how they were holding up since her brother's death. She said it had been very tough, and that her mom, dad, and brother Sony had been barely holding it together. She said that Sony had gone on the wrong path after High school and joined the neighborhood Latin gang, 12th Ave Mafia, and that he was one of the leaders and was doing all sorts of crazy stuff including robberies, selling drugs, etc. She said that she was always afraid that what he was doing would somehow threaten her safety and the safety of her parents, but he didn't seem to care. She then asked me how I was doing, what I'd been up to, and how my parents and family was doing, mainly just small talk. I said everything with me was great, that I'd been married and divorced since I'd graduated from college, and that I was just working and enjoying life. I asked her if she was now or had been married, or if she was seeing anyone. She said she had never gotten married, and that she had been seeing someone, but that he was too immature for her and for her current situation. I asked what situation she was referring to, and she smiled and said I would find out later. At that point I was very curious as to what she was talking about, but I figured I would find out at some point and so I didn't press the issue.

At that point the alcohol started to take affect and we became more relaxed, we became a little more comfortable, and the conversation started to get a little deeper as we started to talk about the old days in the Park, about Corey, about her and Corey, about why we hadn't kept in contact, and about her brother Caesar. I then asked her what she remembered about that night, as I hadn't really had a chance to talk to her about it before. She said that the whole day was as clear in her mind as if it had just happened the day before. She told me how she and Corey had planned out their day, and had planned to be together at her house when she knew no-one would be home. She said that everything had gone perfectly with their plan, and that it was the best day of her life. She said that after she and Corey made love, they lay there in her bed in each other's arms and just talked. They talked about their lives, their families, their plans to be together for the rest of their lives, and their love for each other. As she spoke, I could see that she was starting to get emotional. Her eyes began to water, and her voice began to crack a little. The wounds of what had happened still cut her and had never completely healed. I took her hand as she continued to talk, and I couldn't help noticing how soft it was. This was where my ability to be a true friend would be tested, and I just continued to hold her hand as she went on. She said that on that night, as they laid there, still a little buzzed from the weed they had smoked, they didn't hear her brother come in the front door, and that when he knocked on her door, it startled them, and Corey quickly and quietly jumped to his feet and put his clothes on. They didn't know if he was just knocking to check or if he would try to come in, and when he asked who was in there with her, Corey quickly jumped into the closet. She said that she then tried to get rid of her brother as quickly as possible, and when the phone rang and he went to answer it, Corey came out of the closet, quietly opened her window, they kissed, he told her he loved her and that he'd call her when he got home, and jumped out of the window and headed towards the sidewalk. She said that she then lay back down, rolled over for a second just thinking about what had happened, and how happy she was, and then began to doze off for a second before she heard the loud bangs of gunfire. She then said something that went along with what Isaac told us when we'd talked to him. She said that while she was lying there dozing off, she could swear that she remembered hearing Corey talking or arguing with someone, and she remembered thinking that Caesar had caught him jumping out of the window and that they were arguing. She said that it all happened so quickly that she didn't even have time to react to the sounds of the voices before the gunfire erupted, and that immediately after she heard it her first thoughts were of Corey, and once the shooting stopped she jumped to her feet and peeked out of her window to see what going on. She said from there she could see her brother Caesar kneeling over a body lying on the pavement in front of their house. She then heard the sounds of sirens and ran as quickly as she could out to where her brother was. As she ran out of the house, she could see the police car parked in front of her house, and the police officers standing a few feet from her brother as he leaned over the body on the ground. She said the police officers handcuffed Caesar and laid him on his stomach, and she ran over to see who had been shot. In her mind she knew who it was, but in her state of shock she had to see it with her own eyes. She said that as she got closer, her heart began to beat harder and harder and felt like it would pound right through her chest. She said her fears were realized as she arrived at the body and that it was Corey lying there in a pool of his own blood. She said there was a huge hole in his chest that still had smoke coming out of it and that he was not breathing. He was dead, and as she said this she seemed to be looking off into space, thinking and reliving what happened in her mind as though it was happening right then. She started to cry and I hugged and comforted her and started to cry myself. She then said that she remembered screaming at her brother who was sitting on the curb in handcuffs, asking him why he had killed Corey. After that she said everything seems to have been a blur. She remembers the police taking her brother away in the car as her parents drove up, her having to explain to them what was going on, and the crazy things that the neighbors, including Corey's parents were saying to them about Caesar. She said that after that her other brother Sony began to get terrorized at school, and that he joined the gang for protection.

She then said something that was very interesting to me at the time, something that I felt I needed to look into further. She said that even though she couldn't remember much about what happened, it had always bothered her that she did remember that she thought she'd heard Corey talking to someone right before he was shot. She said that she had always thought that it was a figment of her imagination and a side effect of the weed that they had smoked, so she never brought it up. I asked her if she thought it may have been Caesar, and she said no, because at the time things were happening so fast, and she was so distraught about what happened to Corey that she didn't remember until she calmed down a little and had time to think. I asked her if she was sure, and if maybe she was still feeling the effects of the weed, and she said that she was absolutely sure, and that she'd told her brother's attorney as much, thinking it would clear her brother, but he told her that without anyone else to back up her story, it would look like she was just making it up to get her brother off, so he never presented it as evidence. I then asked her if she'd talked to her brother after he'd gotten out of prison or while he was in there, and she said that she went to visit him all the time, and that although she'd thought that he'd killed Corey right when it happened, after she came to her senses she knew that he didn't. She said that her brother's attorney was a joke, and that even though her brother proclaimed his innocence from the beginning, it was his attorney who was the one who convinced him that with the evidence against him he was better off taking a plea and doing 7 years instead of going to trial and probably losing, and doing 20 years.

At that point I heard a car drive up, and Carmen looked me in the eye and said that it was time for me to see the secret that she'd talked about earlier. She then got up, went to the front door and opened it. I could hear her saying hello to someone, and at that point her mom walked in the door, recognized me and said hello. I said hello, asked her how she was doing, and hugged her. Carmen, who'd walked outside, came walking back into the house holding a little boy in her arms. After she placed him down on the ground and he turned around, chills went up and down my spine and the hair on my neck and arms stood up. She told him to introduce himself to me, and he said hello, my name is Corey. I couldn't speak. He looked like he could be Corey's twin. I tried to say hello, but the words barely came out. I tried to hold back the tears, but I could only do it long enough to shake his little hand. After that I quickly turned away as the tears flowed down my face. Carmen asked her mom to take Corey Jr. and to put him to bed, and before he went he reached to shake my hand again. I picked him up and hugged him like I was hugging Corey after not seeing him for a long time. I finally gathered myself, put him back down, and said good night, and that it was nice to meet him. With that, they went off to his room. I told Carmen that I was very happy for her, and happy that she had a piece of Corey to remind her of him. I then told her about me and Caesar's meeting, and that I didn't believe that he killed Corey. I said that I thought Corey and Caesar's murders were connected somehow, and that I was going to be trying to find out the truth about what happened to them. I then asked her if she'd like to help, and she eagerly responded yes before I could get everything I wanted to tell her out of my mouth. My crew was complete.

Carmen and I spent the rest of the evening talking and enjoying each others' company. Just like the old days. We talked about our lives, what we'd been up to since we'd last seen each other, our present lives, and our plans for the future. It was a great time, and I was so happy for the chance to talk to her, and that she would be a part of what we trying to do. I knew it would be very dangerous for her and for all of us for that matter, but I was sure she could handle it.

Before we knew it, it was around midnight, far past my usual bedtime. I didn't care though. It was great seeing and talking to her. As I got up to leave, we hugged, and I told her I would be in contact with her very soon and assured her that I would do everything in my power to find out who killed both Corey and her brother Caesar. I also told her that I would like to go by her parent's house the next day to try and talk to them and some of the neighbors who might still live there to see if they could remember anything about that night that might help, and asked if she thought her parents could handle that. She said that she thought it would be ok but that she thought it might be easier for them and me if she went along, and asked if that would be ok with me. I said sure, of course it would be cool. She thanked me and asked what time I would be picking her up the next day. I said around 11:00 a.m. and she said that would be great. We hugged again, a little tighter this time, and as she looked into my eyes and smiled, I realized that I could actually be more attracted to her than I had let myself think I was, which could mean trouble. She walked me to the door and watched me through her front window as I walked out to my car. She waved to me again, and I drove off into the night.

As I drove home that night I started thinking and wondering who this guy could be that had been talking to Corey right before he was shot. Could it be the same guy that Isaac and his friends saw him with. Was he the person who killed him? If so, how would we find him after all of this time, if he is even still around? If he is around he was obviously smart enough to stay hidden from the police investigation then, and would be even more difficult to find now. I starting thinking that it was time to look closer into the police investigation to see if there was anything or any other suspects that may have been found that would help me with my investigation. For that I would need James's help, but I was already having doubts about him, and to whom his loyalty was really, me as his friend, or that blue wall of brotherhood know as the SPD, Sacramento Police Department. I guessed there was only one way to find out. Once I went down that road however, there was no going back. I would be deep into the shit, all the way up to my neck. I would call him the next day. First thing tomorrow though, I wanted to take a ride over to the park to try and talk to some of the people who might still live on the street that Corey was killed on, to see if any of them might remember anything that they saw or heard that night or anytime since then that might help me to find out what really happened. This is where it was probably going to start getting dangerous. Oak Park had changed a little since I'd left there, along with the rest of the city. Gangs had slowly been moving in from Southern Cal and the Bay area and staking out territory in some of the urban areas of Sacramento. The Bloods had taken over and controlled a huge portion of the drug trade in Oak Park by that time. Carmen's old block and house were smack in the middle of their territory. I would have to tread very lightly because no-one really knew me over there and some of those who did and remembered me, may feel that I was no longer a part of their neighborhood and may not be willing to tell me anything. Q was not available to go with me. I would take Carmen up on her offer to go with me and to swing by her parents who still lived there. People on their street might be more willing to talk if she was with me. We planned to go over there at around 11:00 a.m. and to get in and out of there before anyone knew we were over there asking questions. You know what they say though. The best laid plans often go awry, and sometimes, they can just get you killed.

BACK TO THE PARK

When I got up the next day I was a little nervous about going over to Oak Park. I hadn't been there in a while, so although I was anxious to see how everything looked and to check out the neighborhood I grew up in, I was still worried about the bad things I'd been hearing about the area since I'd left. I was going with Carmen, and although her parents still lived there, if something were to go down, I would be stuck. I decided to take my piece with me just in case, the .22, not the Nina.

I arrived at Carmen's place to pick her up at around 11:00. She was looking lovely and I made sure to tell her as she got into my car. She had on some really short, tight, white jean shorts and some tan sandals. She also had on a tight tan tank top that matched her sandals. It was going to be tough concentrating on the road let alone what we were planning to do once we got over to her parents' house. Our plan was to first talk to her mom and dad to see if they remembered anything that they'd heard over the years that might help us, or, if they'd talked to Caesar before he was killed. We would then try to talk to any of the neighbors that were around at the time that Corey was killed to see if they knew of or had heard anything that might help us.

As I drove up 12th Ave and arrived at 33rd street, I began to reminisce about the great times that me and my friends had while growing up there. I could see that Oak Park Market, although it had changed a bit, was still there. I should have taken a left on 33rd to get to 10th Avenue where the Martinez family lived, but I took a right on 33rd just to see how much had changed on the street where I grew up. The houses were of course a little older looking and there were people that I didn't recognize as I slowly drove down the street, but other than that, nothing had changed. It was funny, I actually felt like I was home. As I rode down the street I stopped for a moment in front of my old house which was across from the market. I could almost hear us playing down the street with our friends, laughing, capping on each other, playing hide and go seek, freeze tag or something, talking about nothing in particular, without a care in the world, and my mom calling us to come in the house as it was starting to get late. Our old house had an alley on one side, which had separated our place from Y&W Beauty supply, which was no longer there. As I cruised a little further down the street I saw the houses of the people I grew up with, thinking, I wonder who was still there, who was gone, who was still alive, and who has passed away. I passed by Q's families house, a house that was pretty much my second home, and then I came to the end of the block. As I rolled around the corner, a painful memory of something very traumatic that happened to us as children came back to me and I felt a sense of deep sadness that I hadn't expected. It was as though the memory of what happened had suddenly began to resurface from deep in the recesses of my mind and come back. I could feel a rush of emotion well up inside of me, and I felt a few tears welling up in my eyes as I turned the corner and passed by Herman's Market, which I was surprised to see was still there. Carmen asked me what was wrong and I told her that I was just thinking of my two friends who were killed at that corner by a drunk driver and that it had flashed through my mind when I turned the corner. She said that Q had told her something about that before, but he really didn't know much about what happened and that he just knew the boys who were killed. I told her that I remembered it just like it was yesterday, because they were two of my closest friends at that time. One of them, Donny, lived on 33rd, and the other one Tray, was in my class at Bret Hart Elementary.

It all happened on a beautiful summer day back in the summer of 1972, right before the start of school. A few of our friends had come to ask me and Ace to come outside and play and we asked my mom if we could, but she told us no, because we needed to get cleaned up to go over our grandmothers that day. When we got home from our grandmothers later that day some of our friends came and knocked on our door. I could remember opening the door, and all of them having a look of terror and anguish on their faces. I asked them what was wrong and that is when they told me. Donny and Tray, who were 8 and 10 years old at the time, had been hit by a car at the end of the block. Tray had come to our block to hang out, and he and Donny were chasing one of our other friends down the street on their bikes. The kid that they were chasing had already rounded the corner and was way ahead of them, so they had to ride as fast as they could to catch him. Q, who was one of the kids that was telling me what happened, said that he was outside of his house on his bike as they passed, and they shouted for him to join them as they passed. He said that he jumped on his bike to follow them, but as he started to ride, he fell off his bike in the gutter. That is when he heard and saw what happened. As the two boys were turning the corner on their bike, a car that was coming from around the corner on the wrong side of the street struck both of them, first Tray and then Donny, causing them to fly off their bikes and hit the street. Q said that he couldn't believe how high they flew in the air when they were hit and how loud it sounded when the car struck them. Tray died instantly, and Donny was unconscious and bleeding heavily. When they first told me I thought they were just messing with me and my brother to get us to come outside, but just looking at their faces I realized they were telling the truth. I remember thinking to myself, how could this happen on our street. How could this happen to two people who I knew so well and was so close to? Nothing like this had ever happened to me, or on our street. The beautiful summer day suddenly had become gloomy and dark. I couldn't even go to sleep that night thinking of my two friends. Donny lasted for another week in the hospital, but died from his injuries. Since we were so young, my mother wouldn't let us go to the funerals for fear of the effect it might have on us. It didn't work though. It still had a very deep effect on all of us who grew up together on our street. The loss of Donny had a lasting effect on all of us and seemed to bring us all closer together and made us value each other more somehow. It had an effect on me personally for a long time, and I still have thoughts and dreams of both of them at times.

We continued on our way to the Martinez place and got there at around 11:30 a.m. Both Edgar and Lola seemed to have gotten nicer than I'd remembered them being growing up. They told us to sit with them in their living room and asked if I would like something cool to drink like water or ice tea, and I told them that water would be fine. As we sat down I expressed my condolences for the loss of their son, and went on to tell them how he'd contacted me to meet him on the night that he was killed, and told them what he'd told me. I then asked them if he'd told them anything about meeting me that night, or, about anything that he wanted to talk to me about. They both said that they really didn't know what he had planned to tell me, but Lola did tell me that before he left the house to meet me that night he told her that he was going to straighten everything out, and that he would be talking to someone that would be able to help him clear his name, their family name, and to bring honor back to their family. She said she asked him who he would be meeting and he said that he would be meeting me and that he would be telling me everything and hopefully be able to convince me to help him. Tears starting to form in Edgar's eyes and slowly roll down his face and he spoke for the first time since we had gotten there. He said that after that, they never spoke to their son again. The wounds and hurt of losing their son were still fresh, and I hated stirring up the terrible memories, so I apologized to them for bringing it up, but I promised them both that I would be looking into what happened to both Corey and Caesar. I told them that wherever path my quest for the truth leads me down, I hope that I am able to fulfill their son's promise to clear both his name and the name of their family. Carmen then hugged both of her parents and I was surprised that they also hugged me. We walked towards the door to leave, and before we walked out, Carmen's mother gently took both of my hands in hers and said that she would pray for my safety while on my journey for the truth, and asked if I would please watch out for her daughter and keep her safe. I told her that I would do everything I could to do what she requested, and with that we walked out of the door.

Our next stop on the block would be to the Martinez's next-door neighbor Mrs. Wilma White, who was the longest resident of the street and who the police reports said was watching TV in her living room on the night that Corey was shot, and who said she heard shots just before police arrived on the seen to find Caesar kneeling over Corey. She was very old by this time, probably in her mid 80s, but hopefully she would be willing to talk to us and let us know if she remembered anything else that may help us figure out what really happened. Before we walked up to the door Carmen mentioned that she remembered that Mrs. White was always pretty salty and grumpy towards everyone, and I said yes I kind of remember that and that she would probably be even worse now. She said that she was never like that towards her though, and that she'd always been nice to her, and that it would probably be a good idea to let her do the talking once she answered the door. I agreed as we walked up to the door and I rang the doorbell. After ringing the bell for a second time we thought she may not be there, and started to walk off. Just then we heard a faint crackly voice asking who's there. Carmen said it's me Mrs. White, Carmen. Mrs. White then asked in a slightly louder and irritated sounding voice, who? Carmen then said in a slightly louder voice, it's me, Carmen from next door. The door slowly began to open and once it finally did, there stood Mrs. White, who hadn't changed all that much, accept for the fact she'd gotten a few years older. She had on a thick dark purple robe and house slippers and I remember wondering how she could stand to be in such a thick robe on such a warm summer day. As she opened her screen door the look of anger that had been on her face turned to a smile as she saw that it was Carmen. She hugged her and told her how good it was to see her, and asked us to come in to sit with her in her living room.

Once inside I could see why she had on the thick robe. She had her air conditioner blasting and it was freezing cold in there. As we took a seat on her couch, she sat across from us in a big old comfortable looking lounge chair. Carmen asked her if she remembered me from back in the day, and after looking at me for a second or two with a kind of confused look on her face as if she were trying to remember, she said yes, that she did remember me, but that she didn't remember my name. She said that she remembered me as one of the kids that used to hang around with Corey. She then went on to say that it was such a shame what happened to him, and that it was also a shame that Caesar had gone to prison for killing when he hadn't done it. After hearing this Carmen and I looked at each other with complete surprise, and Carmen asked Mrs. White why she said Caesar didn't kill Corey and how she knew this. Mrs. White said that at first she had thought he had killed Corey, but after a while and after having a chance to think about it, she knew he didn't, because before she heard the gunshots that night, she heard two people arguing in front of the house, one a man and the other that sounded more like a young man or teenager, and as she went to see who it was, the gunshots rang out causing her to hit the floor for fear of being hit. She said that immediately after the shots were fired she heard a car quickly drive away, and when she got back to her feet, she looked out her window, saw a body lying there, and then saw Caesar run up to the body, and check to see if the person was still alive. She said that Caesar had a gun in his hand when he ran up to the body, and at that moment she just assumed he had shot whoever it was. She said that after she had thought about it for a while, and after finding out it was a teenage boy that had gotten shot, she began to think that maybe it wasn't Caesar who had done the shooting and that maybe it was whomever she had heard arguing with Corey right before the shots rang out. I asked her why she'd never come forward to share this information with the police or with Caesar's attorney, and she said that she had, and they said they checked into it and that it wasn't relevant to the case. She said that they'd told her that if they needed her to testify, they would contact her, but they never did. I asked her if she remembered the officer or officers that she had talked to in regards to the information that she just told us, and she said that she believed the one of the officer's names was Cool, James Cool. On hearing this, a cold feeling ran through my body. I looked at Carmen and told her we had to go. She said why, what's up? I said I would tell her a little later, but that we had to go. As we stood up, Mrs. White hugged Carmen and then me, and said how good it was to see us and to see that we had both grown up to be such fine young adults. She said that she hoped we would stay together for a long time, to which we both quickly corrected her to say we are just friends and that we are just working together to see if we could find out what really happened to Corey. She said that she would always remember Corey because he was always such a nice and polite young man, and that when he saw her in her front yard as he passed by, he would always smile and ask her how she was doing, and if she needed help with anything. She said it was nothing like the other kids who lived around there then. They were all so rude and disrespectful. She said she hoped we could find what we were looking for, and if we needed her to tell her story to anyone to let her know. We both thanked her and headed out the door. As we walked to the car I told Carmen about James and the fact that he was supposed to be helping us with finding out information, but that now I was starting to have suspicions about him and that we would have to be careful about what we told him and said around him until I could find out what was up.

Before we headed home I told Carmen I wanted to walk back over to 33rd to Corey's parent's house to see how they were doing and to see if they might remember anything from that night. I told her it might be a better idea if I went by myself and she said that she understood. I told her I would probably not be very long, to wait at her parents' house and I would come back to get her. The reason that I told her that it might be better if I go to the Jenkins house by myself was that even though it had been 7 years since Carmen's brother confessed to killing Corey, the wounds were probably still there, and since his murder they had always blamed Carmen and his relationship with her for being the cause of his death. They felt that if their son had never gotten involved with her, he would still be alive, and everyone, including me until this point, had agreed with them.

I slowly walked up the street towards the Jenkins' house, wondering how they would react towards me when I told them that I didn't think that Caesar had killed Corey, and asking them questions that would open old wounds that had probably just started to heal. It was going to be tough, they might resent me for believing Caesar and Carmen, and even though I had been close to the family at one time and still felt I was, things could very well get pretty bad based on how I handled the situation, and the future of my relationship with them might never be the same.

As I walked up to the door I began to feel anxious and uncomfortable, not really knowing what I was going to say. I rang the doorbell and no-one answered. Maybe I had gotten lucky and no-one was home. I rung the bell again, half hoping no-one would answer this time either, but just as I started to turn to walk away, Mr. Jenkins opened the door, and a big smile came over his face. He said, what's up Perry, long time no see, put his arms around me and gave me a big bear hug. He took my arm and told me to come in, and as we walked into the house he called for Mrs. Jenkins. She came from the other room and with a big smile on her face said, Perry, oh my God it is so good to see you. She looked a little smaller and older since the last time I'd seen her. They both did. I heard they had reconciled after being broken up for a while after Corey died, and it was nice to see that they were back together again. Mr. Jenkins asked how I'd been since the last time they've seen me and I told them that I was doing well and told them about my job. They asked how my parents were doing and I told them that my mom was fine but that my father had passed away the past year. They expressed their condolences for my loss and told me to send my mom their love and to tell her that their prayers were with her. I asked them how everything was with them, and how the family was doing and they said everything was good, and that everyone was doing well. Mrs. Jenkins then asked what I was doing in the neighborhood, and I suddenly got a lump in my throat. I knew I had to do what I'd come there to do however, so I said that I was there trying to find out some information so that I could look into what really happened to Corey. There was a deafening silence for a moment, and they both looked at each other, and then looked at me with a strange, confused look on their faces. Mr. Jenkins was the first to respond to what I said.

What? What do you mean you are looking into what happened to Corey? Are you out of your mind or something?

I said, "No sir, I am not out of my mind."

I then explained to them about what Caesar told me, and all of the things that we had been uncovering that seemed to point to the fact that the wrong person went to prison for Corey's murder, and that I just wanted to check into it to see what really happened. Mrs. Jenkins slowly sat down on the couch with her head down, and after a few seconds she looked up at me and said,

"We already know who killed my son, we sat there in the courtroom and listened to him confess it, and now you are coming around here telling us that you don't think he did it because of something that he told you? How could this be? We thought Corey was your friend."

I said

"Yes ma'am, Corey was my friend, one of my closest friends, and that is why I'm doing what I'm doing, because I want to find out the truth about what happened. If it turns out that I am wrong, and Caesar was the one that killed him, then in the end he got what he deserved, but if I am right, and Corey's murderer is still out there somewhere, I need to find him and bring him to justice."

With that, Mrs. Jenkins stood up and walked out of the room to the kitchen. I then told Mr. Jenkins that I was sorry for opening old wounds, but that I thought I should come and tell them before I proceeded with what I was doing, out of respect to them. At that point Mr. Jenkins said that it would probably be best if I left, and he walked me to the front door. Once outside I apologized again, and he said that it was ok and even though he thought I was wrong, he understood why I was doing what I was doing. He then hugged me and told me to stay safe and to please let them know if I find out anything. I told him that they would be the first ones I would contact either way.. As I walked away and watched him walk back into the house, I felt really bad inside. Whatever I had started I'd better follow it through until the end, I owed them that and I owed Corey that. I only prayed to God that what my mind was telling me was right, for my sake and for theirs.

As I turned on to 10th street and walked back towards Carmen's parents' house I could see that there were 4 dudes who looked like they might be looking for trouble standing by my car, one of them actually sitting on it. As I approached them, Carmen came out to meet me, and as we met I whispered to her asking if she knew them. She said that she knew two of them and that they were two brothers who lived on the street. She said she didn't know the others, but that they were probably members of her brother's gang. I had already moved my Nina from the small of my back to the front of my pants and untucked my shirt to hide it, just in case things got hot, but I was hoping they knew Carmen and would be cool. If not, I had to be ready to start blasting. As we arrived at the car I said what up to all of them and asked if they had seen Sony. One of the brothers responded

"What's up Homey, Na, we ain't seen Sony, what set you claiming?"

I responded,

"I ain't claiming no set, I just came by with my friend to visit her parents."

The other brother said

"Is Carmen your girl?"

I said

"No, she's just a friend of mine that I grew up with when I lived around the corner from here on 33rd, back in the day."

The other brother said I didn't look like anyone he had ever seen around there, and I said that was because it was a long time ago, probably before he moved over there. He then said

"Just because you with Carmen and used to live around here don't mean you can just come back around our block and hang out whenever you want, unless you want to pay the toll."

I said

"The toll?"

"Yeah the toll."

"What's the toll?"

"It depends".

"Depends on what?"

"It depends if you want to walk out of here without your car, or crawl out of here without your car. If you want to walk out, it will cost you $20.00. If you want to crawl out, it will only be $10.00."

I said,

"How much if I want to drive out with my car?"

"Oh, that would be $50."

The others laughed and I could tell Carmen was getting scared. After a few moments of silence, the guy asked which it would be. This wasn't going at all like I'd planned. I was hoping we could get in and get out of there without any trouble, but as usual for me, that wasn't the case. The problem for these guys was that they had made a huge mistake. They took me for someone who they'd caught off guard, weak and afraid, and an easy target. In other words they let the smooth taste fool them. Because of this error in their judgment, they were not really prepared for what I might do if I were not what they thought I was. If they had been, they would have drawn their guns before they started making demands and trying to get my money. It was a mistake they were getting ready to pay a heavy price for. Before they knew what was happening, I pulled my Nina out of the front of my pants, hit the two of them standing next to me in the back of their heads with the butt of the gun, knocking them to the ground. I then quickly grabbed the one who was doing all of the talking by his hair, and pointed the gun to the back of his head. I then calmly said,

"I think Ima take the 4th option, the one where me and my friend get in my car and drive away."

At that point it was a stalemate and I didn't know what to do next. Just then, one of them asked if I was sure I wanted to talk to Sony, and I said yeah I am sure, and to just tell him to get in contact with me as soon as possible, it was about his brother.

He said,

"I don't think I am going to have to tell him to do that."

I looked at him and said,

"You don't think you have to do that, and why is that?"

He said,

"Why don't you turn around and you can ask him yourself."

My heart immediately began to beat through my chest, and a cold feeling took over my body. Both Carmen and I slowly turned around and there standing behind us as big as life was Sony. He looked a little older and a lot harder, but he still had a baby face and cold blue eyes. After looking coldly at me for a few seconds, he finally spoke.

What's up P? and then reached to shake my hand. I didn't know what to do at that point, but with the odds being as they were at the time, I decided to take a calculated chance, so I removed the gun from the back of the dudes head, and reached to shake Sony's hand. After we shook hands, he looked at Carmen and said in a sarcastic tone, what's up sis. You come to see moms and pops? Carmen just looked at him and didn't say anything. He just stood there for a second, no expression on his face, no words coming out of his mouth, just staring at me up and down, with those cold blue eyes. After looking at me for a few more seconds, he said,

"So what's up with you P, what you doing over on this side of town? I heard you moved on up in the world like George Jefferson."

The other dudes started to laugh, and so did I. I told him that I was over there trying to find out who really killed Corey. He looked over at Carmen again and without changing his facial expression or the tone of his voice, he said, what's up sis, did you go in to see moms and pops? She looked back at him with a kind of disgusted look on her face and said, in a kind of sarcastic tone, yes, I just came out of the house. He then came back at her saying,

"Well I know you definitely didn't come to see me,"

and then looked at his homies and started laughing, causing them all to start laughing also. I tried to let out a little laugh, but it sounded totally fake and they all stopped and looked at me like I was crazy. He then said, so after all of this time, and all of the shit that me and my family have been through, now someone wants to come and try to find out what really happened to Corey. He then said,

"Where were you when all them dudes was beating the shit out of me for something my brother did way back when it happened, or when my parents were harassed and threatened by everyone in the neighborhood over what happened. Where were you then P?"

I didn't have an answer for him. All I could say was,

"Hey Man, I am sorry for what you and your family went through but there was nuthin I could do back then, but there is something that I want to try to do now, something about what happened to Corey, and something about what happened to your brother Caesar."

He then looked at me for a few more seconds, and finally cracked a smile and said good luck, I hope you find what the fuck you looking for, Corey was a cool little dude.

He then reached out his hand and we shook again. After that, he stared at the dude that I'd knocked off of my car, and yelled at him to get the fuck out of there. The dude quickly jumped up and stumbled over to where the others were standing. He yelled at the others for them to get the fuck out the way so we could get in the car. We got in, and before we drove off, he came over to my side and said that I might want to get out of the park because it didn't have to even get dark nowadays for shit to pop off, especially if folks don't know you. He then said for me to make sure I didn't let anything happen to his sister and that he would be around if I needed him, and with that I drove off. I felt myself take a deep breath as we drove away and I could hear Carmen do the same. We looked at each other, seemingly knowing what the other was thinking, took a few more deep breaths, and in unison, let out sighs of relief followed by laughter, feeling as though we'd just escaped with our lives, and perhaps we had.

I thought all weekend about what Mrs. White had said about James, and also about the fact that he'd never told me that he was the one who'd taken Caesar down to the station that night. Had I put my trust in the wrong person? Was he somehow involved in Corey's murder, or covering up for the person who had actually done it? If so, how would I try to find out without tipping him off. At this point I had to tread very lightly, keep all of my cards close to my chest, and not trust anyone other than the two people I knew I could trust with my life, Face and Carmen.

BLACK PANTHERS VERSUS SAC PD

When I talked to Face about James we agreed that the best thing to do would be to allow him to continue helping us, but not let him know about what we'd found out about him. We also wouldn't fully trust anything that he told us that we couldn't find proof for ourselves. If it became necessary, or if the time came where it was needed, we would both confront him with what we knew, and see what was up. We needed to be very careful though. If he were not being honest with us, and if he was giving us false or misleading information, there had to be a reason for him doing it, so we would need to be very sure of that reason and our facts before we confronted him. After all, he was someone who I had grown to consider to be a friend, and was someone who I thought we could trust. I had always been a flawless judge of people and could see through fakes when I first met them. James never registered on my fake radar. He came off as being a real, honest dude, and if it were to come to pass that he was somehow involved in Corey's death, and Caesar going to prison, everything that I had ever thought about my gift would suddenly be called into question and it would probably affect my confidence in my ability to read people causing a skill that I had counted on my entire life. It I really needed to find out, especially with the stakes being so high at that time.

The first thing to do would be to meet with James to find out if he had any information for me, and to see if I could try to read him again. So I called him that Sunday night, and asked him to meet me at Luigi's pizza the next day to update me on anything he may have found out. I also called Q and asked him if he would also meet with us. I told him that I didn't really trust my ability to read James and I may have made a mistake in trusting him and having him help us. I told him that I needed him to help me talk to him and try to find out if he is really on the up and up and trying to help us, or if he had some alternative motive for being involved in what we were trying to do, and if so help me to find out what it was. Q agreed to help me out and we all met the next day at Luigi's Pizza on Stockton Blvd for lunch the next day. I figured if we met there relatively early, like around 11:00 a.m..

The next day I picked up Q and we headed over to Luigi's to meet up with James. After picking him up, I began telling him what I'd found out about James, and what my concerns now were after finding these things out. He then said that he'd had these concerns all along, but because he knew that I was always right on as far as reading people and knowing where they were coming from, he had never said anything because he figured I had it covered. I told him that this is one time where I may have slipped up and that at lunch I would need him to help me check James out to decide whether he was completely in with us, against us, or whether he had some other motive all together. He agreed and said that it would be like old times where we used teamwork with dealing with outer people, whether it was talking to girls, or getting into fights. We always worked with each other and were there to help the other out whatever the situation. We had each others back. I said, yeah, just like that time when we went to the drive in with those two older babes and their boyfriends drove up on us and wanted to fight. He smiled, laughed, and said yeah, like that, but I don't want to talk about that stuff, and we both starting laughing.

When we drove up to Luigi's I could see that James's car was already there, he was actually there in one of the Department's undercover vehicles, but I knew it was him because those cars can be spotted from a mile away if you know what you are looking for. As we walked in the front door I could see James sitting at one of the tables near the back, and Q and I joined him. We all shook each others hands, exchanged pleasantries, and ordered one of the house specials, a large pepperoni pizza with extra sauce and cheese, and 3 grape sodas. I asked James if he had found out any information for me and he said he had. He said he had been looking through police files in regards to Corey's murder and that he'd found out some very interesting information about one of the officers that was on duty in the area that night. He said that the officer was an undercover officer who had been on duty in the area for about a month to try to find out about some robberies of small stores and liquor stores in the area over a few months. He said that that night was the first night that the officer was placed back on active duty after he had been relieved of duty for several months while the Department was looking into an incident that he was involved in where he and another officer chased down, shot and killed a teen they suspected of being involved robberies the prior year. He said the officers' actions had been deemed justifiable after the Internal Affairs investigation and it was the first night that he was back on duty in the area and that he'd been assigned to do the same thing that he'd been doing before, cruising the area in an undercover car in his civilian clothes. He went on to say that the interesting thing was, that when the call went out saying officers in need of assistance as the crowd gathered at the scene, all cars in the area, including black and whites and undercover, should respond immediately and he was the only one that didn't show up. The file went on to say that the reason he gave that he hadn't shown up, was that his car was having trouble starting and by the time he had gotten it to start, he got the call that the situation had been brought under control so he just went on with his patrol. James said that the funny thing was when the officer got his car back to the garage, he never said anything about having trouble with it. The other thing is, when asked later why he didn't get to the scene in time, he said that he started to head over to the scene, but that his car died on the way, which was different than what he'd previously said. I asked what the officer's name was and he said his name was Michael O'Sullivan, and that his name was well known in police circles because he'd come from a long line of officers including his dad Pete O'Sullivan and his grandfather. I thanked him and told him that it was great information he'd given us, and that I know how risky and dangerous it was for him to get this information for me. He said that it wasn't really any risk involved, and that if I wanted him to actually talk to Michael to find out anything, he would be happy to do it. I said I would let him know. I then decided it would be a good time to let Q ask him some question that would help us with some of the concerns we had in regards to him because that is what he was good at, and I felt it would be better if I observed because that is what I was good at. Just like old times.

Q began by saying how lucky I was to have a friend like James, and asked James if he was at all concerned about other officers finding out that he was helping us and then retaliating against him for betraying that fraternity they called the blue shield? He also asked him if he thought about the fact it could affect their trust in him to have their backs, and if he worried about the safety of his family, and that he could be putting his life and their lives in danger by helping us. James said yes, he'd thought about all that, but he then went on to say that he himself had also come from a family of police officers, including his father, and that he had always been told by his father something he would never forget and that he would always live by. He said his father told him that once he became a police officer, he became a part of a brotherhood, a brotherhood that is protected by a blue shield, and that it was his duty to always protect and stay true to that shield. He said his father then went on to say that protecting that shield did not mean that you should look the other way when your brothers or fellow police officers do something wrong, because that would not be keeping the shield strong or protecting it. He said that their wrong doing, and any officer who helped them or covered up their wrong doing, weakens the shield, and that and officer's obligation is to protect and serve the public, and to help those who call and rely on you for help. He said there will always be those people who will cuss you, or hate you, just because you are a police officer, and that is something you will have to deal with from time to time, but for the most part, people have comfort in knowing you are there, and will always call you when they need you to help them with something that is out of their control. James also said that he really has a deep hatred for bad cops because not only do they make the good cops look bad, they also are betraying the trust of those people who put them in place to protect those who cannot protect themselves.

With that, Q looked at me and we both nodded our heads in agreement. There were no further questions that were necessary. We had not only been lucky enough to find a good cop to help us but I also realized that I had found a good friend, something that was rare, and that should be cherished, valued and appreciated once it is found. Once as we grow older we realize that a real friend will always be there for us throughout our entire life, never judging, never criticizing, never back stabbing, but there, through thick and thin, through good times and bad, they will always be there, and that is what I had always had in Q and what I knew I now had in James. Our pizza and grape sodas came, we ate our lunch, and enjoyed the rest of our time talking about shit that guys always talk about, sports, women, politics, and women. It was great, but now we had to take the information that James had given us to add to the puzzle and to try to put things together and find some answers. Before he left I asked James if he could do me one more favor and meet with Michael O'Sullivan to try and see if he could find out anything else about him that he could. I told him to be very careful and to really keep it casual and to try not to alert him about anything. He agreed and told me he would see what he could find out. With that we all shook hands and left.

While driving Q home I told him that maybe we could go and talk to our friend Big Boy Patterson who may know something about Michael O'Sullivan's father from back in the days when he was a Black Panther, and find out if he had any dealings he may have had with him. I told Q that maybe I should talk to Big Boy on my own since he didn't like him because he thought he used to see his daughter Korryn behind his back. Q said it was cool and he could come with me and that Big Boy didn't trip off of that anymore. I couldn't believe he ever did mess with her. When he first told me about it while he was seeing her, I told him that he was crazy and that if Big Boy ever found out to not count on me for backup because Big Boy is crazy and a stone killer, and would kill both of us instead of just him. But Q, being who he was at the time, just couldn't resist because his daughter, who was the same age as us, was fine as hell, and he just had to have her. It didn't last long, and ended once she went away to school, but during the time they were seeing each other I was always nervous around Big Boy because I knew that if he ever found out what was going on, he would be looking to kill Q, which would have meant that I would have had to get involved, and that it would probably end up bad for both of us. They almost got caught a few times and Big Boy threatened Q for being around the house or even on the block several times, but nothing ever really jumped off. I think Big Boy kind of knew they had messed around even if he never had proof, but since he really didn't know for sure, all he ever really did was make threats that I was so happy he never followed through on. Q was crazy for messing with that girl back then, and he was crazy now for thinking Big Boy was cool with him, but if he thought he could talk to him I had no problem with that. So we planned to go and talk to him the next day.

As I said before, Big Boy Patterson was a stone killer who received his training while during two tours of duty in Vietnam, the first by way of the draft, and the second by way of being a volunteer. He was trained as a sniper and was given medals for the kills that he made with his rifle. He was the top marksmen in the service at one time and had one trophy for contests he'd one during the time he was in there. He was eventually dishonorably discharged however for choking out his commanding officer for what was rumored as a comment that he made about black servicemen. Supposedly, while in the officer's club one night, the officer had had a little to much to drink and was hanging out with his buddies. Big Boy had also had a few that night, and was also in the club talking to a couple of the young ladies who had come there, a couple of them being white. Well, I guess the officer didn't like this and decided to show off for his buddies by trying to embarrass Big Boy and his other friend he was with at the time. As Big Boy excused himself from the table he had been sharing with the young ladies to go to the restroom, he passed by the table that the officer and his friend were at, and the office decided to make a comment loud enough for Big Boy and everyone to hear. Something to the effect of Niggers should be happy that white people let them fight in the war, and that if it were up to him he would send all of them back home to work in the field like they should be doing. Big Boy, unaffected by the fact that the guy had bars on his sleeve, responded by saying that is not where he would be if he were back home. The officer said, oh really, and where would you have your black ass if you wasn't in the fields picking cotton, somewhere robbing a store or trying to fuck one of your cousins. Marcus smiled, looked at the guy's friends, and then looked straight into his eyes and said, na, I would be over at your house having a threesome with your wife and your mom while you and your daddy is working in the field. The club patrons broke out in laughter completely embarrassing the officer, who turned as red as a tomato. Big Boy started to head towards the restroom, but when he turned to leave the officer immediately grabbed him by the arm and before his friends could stop him. That was a mistake however, as Big Boy, acting on instinct, immediately spun out of the officer's grip, and grabbed him in a headlock and choke hold. Big Boy knew he would be in big trouble if he did to the officer what he actually wanted to do, so he told the officer to calm down and he would let him out of the headlock, and it seemed as though he did, so he let him go. Once he was let go however, the officer immediately spat in Big Boy's face and then slapped him calling him a stupid nigger. Well, he shouldn't have done that because in doing that he took Big Boy to a place that most people who knew him knew not to take him. A place of almost hypnotic, uncontrollable anger and rage where he has no idea what he does, and has no control of himself, and a place where whoever or whatever is responsible for his anger suffers the usually immediate and dire repercussions and pain of his wrath. Once at this place, there is no stopping him from exacting on the unfortunate party who has caused him to go there, and anyone who tries to stop him will get the same if not worse treatment that the person he is focused on. The officer caught a break however because once he spat in his face, the script of what would happen had already been written, and before he could finish and could get the N in nigger out of his mouth, Big Boy hit him in the jaw so quick and so hard that it sounded like a loud smack and dull thud of someone hitting a slab of meat with a sledge hammer when he connected with his jaw. The officer went flying through the air and over the bar, and he was out before he hit the floor. Big Boy then looked at the officer's friends who were both amazed and petrified at this point, looked at the ladies and said, y'all ready to get out of here. They all shook their heads yes, and they left. The officer's friends rushed to their friend who was out cold on the other side of the bar, and they had the bartender call the paramedics and the MPs. Big Boy was arrested the next day, and when he went before the military court they gave him two options without even listening to his side of the story, go to jail, or take a dishonorable discharge. He told them that he would choose the dishonorable discharge not because he wanted to take the easier route, but because he joined the service to fight for a country he thought would honor him as a hero and treat him as such, but if they didn't want to even hear his side of the story, then he didn't want to serve anymore, and that he felt a black soldier would never be honored anyway. He was dishonorably discharged from the service in 1970, moved back to 33rd street in Oak Park with his mom, his grandmother, and two brothers, and after a 2 year stint in prison for armed robbery, he joined a group of militants that he thought shared some of the same views he had about the white establishment and the harassment and mistreatment of Blacks by law enforcement, the Black Panthers. After 6 months with the Panthers however, Big Boy, was deemed to be to violent and dangerous, and they kicked him out. After that he joined the Black Muslims who had also began to organize in the area, and because of his military and combat skills, and his ability to use firearms, he was assigned as one of the fruits of Islam, who were created to help defend the members of the Nation of Islam and all others. That didn't last very long either as he was also asked to leave them once again because he had anger control issues, he was resistant to authority, and because he was to violent. After leaving the Muslims, he met and married his wife Isabel, and they had three daughters including the one Q had fooled around with, Korryn. Married life seemed to settle him down, and he became more mellow as he got older, accept for when it comes to anyone messing around or doing anything to harm his wife or his daughters, which will bring out the old Big Boy that no-one wants to see or the mess with.

Q and I arrived at Big Boy's place over on 9th Ave in the park at around 3:00 that next day. As we walked up to the porch I again told Q to chill and let me do the talking, and he reluctantly agreed. As I reached to ring the doorbell however Q quickly beat me to it and rang it over and over again until someone quickly and loudly opened the door. It was Big Boy, and he slung the door and screen open and quickly stepped out on to the porch. He yelled in my face, what the fuck you fools ringing my bell like that for, you crazy? I don't think he recognized me at first, and once he did, the scowl that he had on his face kind of went away, and his voice and tone went down a little. He then smiled and grabbed me around the neck in a chokehold and said what up P, where you been hiding out at? I knew it was cool then, at least for me. He then looked over at Q, who smiled and reached out to shake his hand. Q, speaking as if everything was everything between the two of them, said what up big boy, how you been doing man? Big Boy let go of my neck, and with the scowl back on his face, stared into Q's eyes never reaching out to shake his hand, and as if never hearing Q's question, said, what you niggas want. Q quickly shook his own hand and took a step back realizing that things were not as good between the two of them as he thought.

I began to ask Big Boy a few questions about his old days with the Panthers and if he remembered ever running into or having any dealings with cops. He said as a Panther you would always get in beefs and have to deal with the police, and that the main focus of the SPD at that time was pursue and harass any member of the party that they ran across, and to try to provoke a response from them by doing anything that they could to force them into a situation where there could be harassed, arrested, or even killed. He said that he had quite a few run ins with them. I then asked if he remembered having any run ins with an officer named Pete O'Sullivan. He then looked at me with a surprised and somewhat suspicious look on his face and he walked up to within a foot of me and looked into my face as if I were someone he hated from way back in the day. Before I knew what was going on, he grabbed me around my throat with one of his extra large hands, and slammed me up against the wall. His grip around my throat was so tight I couldn't shake myself loose, and he actually had me slightly suspended off the ground. I couldn't breathe, and no matter how hard I tried to move or free my arms up to get to my piece, or to get away and to loosen his grip, I couldn't. Q stepped forward, pulled out a small pistol that I didn't know he'd brought, pointed it at Big Boy's head and told Big Boy to let me go. Big Boy just looked back at him and said he was lucky it wasn't him that he had up there or he'd be dead already. With that, Q released the safety on his gun and pointed it at Big Boy's head again. He then said that if Big Boy didn't let me go in two seconds he would spread his brains all over his nice white door. Big Boy finally let me go and quickly pounced on Q and grabbed him around his neck and slammed him up against the wall. I quickly gathered myself, pulled out my Beretta, pointed it at the back of Big Boy's head, and yelled for him to let Q loose. Big Boy started growling like a dog and laughing. This fool was even crazier than I thought. My hand began to shake as I began to think that I might really have to waste this dude. Thinking quickly I decided to go ahead and answer the question that he had asked us. I said that we were just trying to look into Corey's murder and that we thought that O'Sullivan may have had something to do with it. After a few seconds of silence, Big Boy finally loosened his grip on Q's neck, pushed him over to the side, turned towards me, and with the gun barrel now aimed at his forehead, said, what you want to know? I slowly moved away from him, breathed a sigh of relief, and lowered my gun, never actually putting it away. I then asked him if he could remember ever having any run ins or dealing with Pete O'Sullivan. He said yes, he knew him very well and that he had several run ins with him during that time. He said that O'Sullivan was probably the most racist of all of the police in the area at that time, and that he was one officer that went above and beyond the call of duty to carry out the orders of the SPD to harass all of the Panthers that he ran into because he loved to do it and would do it whenever he could. He didn't care if it were Men, Women or children, he would do whatever he could to harass and terrorize members of the party whenever he could. He then told us that all of that stopped in the summer of 1969. He went on to describe to us in detail about the chain of events that occurred that that we had all always heard about, but never really new much about.

It started on a typically hot day in Oak Park. The temperature had to be at least 100 degrees if not hotter, but the weather was not the only thing that made it hot that day. Local Black Panthers, and others had been clearing people from the street and warning the very young that it wasn't going to be safe on the street that day and that they should go home or they might get hurt, as if they knew something really bad was about to happen. Some of the kids lived too far away to walk home however, so the doors of the BPP were unlocked and the children were told they could stay there for shelter. After the children were safely hidden in the office located on 35th Street, right in the heart of the park, a police patrol car went by with two officers in it. What happened at that point is a source of contention and disagreement between the two sides, but the officers claimed to have been fired at from inside the office, and they in turn returned the fire. The Panthers who were in the office at the time, included Big Boy, contend that the police officers shot three canisters of tear gas through the window which sent choking and blinding fumes throughout the building. He said that they then gathered the children one by one and let them out the back door, which the police had failed to cover. One of the men said that he barely escaped death after he had returned to check for people left in the building saying that he was yanked from the path of police bullets by another Panther. Once the teargas was in the building police entered with gas masks. Some of the officers jumped onto a display case and tore

Panther posters from the wall. Others turned over desks and ripped out wires. They brought out arm-loads of equipment and material. When the officers left the building, it was totally unusable and the teargas effects still hang over the building for 48 hours.

The Panthers say that police harassment continued a month later when the same office was again tear-gassed and fired upon without provocation by a police car that had pulled up and shined its lights through the widow at the front of the office. The officers in the car didn't say anything, they just continued to fire their weapons for what seemed like forever, with a total disregard for if their might be someone in the office that might be hit by their gunfire. One man, who was hit in the shoulder by one of the bullets fired into the building, screamed for everyone, including 4 men and 2 women to get low, and to make their way back to the room in which they kept their own guns, as they made it to the room, they could hear the police car speed off into the night. Their relief however was quickly overcome by horror once the lights were turned on as one of the women, who was well known for her volunteer efforts in the community, and her hard work and love for the kids in the area, and who was 8 months pregnant at the time, lay motionless on the floor with a bullet hole in her forehead.

Two weeks later, while on patrol in the area, a police officer was gunned down by sniper fire. There were four men arrested and charged with his murder and the case. The case which later became known as The Four, was in the papers everyday, and the men were labeled as cop killers in the media. Due to holes in the evidence presented by the DA, and the unreliability of the primary witnesses in the case, the DA dropped the charges and they were freed after 8 months of incarceration. This incident was one of the major incidents along with others that marked the beginning of the end for the Party as many of the Party members felt that it had gotten away from its original mission which was to protect the black community against the brutality and harassment of corrupt and racist law enforcement officers and had become to political. Big Boy then said that the policeman that had been shot and killed was Pete O'Sullivan, and that the Panthers who had been accused and put on trial for his murder were him, Corey's dad Terry Jenkins, Terry Rainwater, and a guy named Daryl Ridgeway. Suddenly all of the pieces of the puzzle were slowly starting to fall in place. We still didn't really know if we had all the pieces that we needed to put the puzzle together however, and find out why and how Corey and Caesar had been murdered. We did have a new possible motive for the murders however, and the list of suspects was starting to become clearer. We were also pretty sure now of what I had already suspected, Caesar had nothing to do with Cory's death and it appeared as though he was used as a scapegoat and to throw everyone off the track of the true killers. .

Even though it had been very difficult to say the least to get the information from Big Boy, the information that we got from him what's the biggest lead that we had gotten so far. Before we left I told Big Boy that I want to thank him for his help and that I apologize if we said or did anything to stir up memories that he wanted to keep buried. I said we were just trying to find out what really happened to our friend I was sure that he would do the same thing if you were in our situation. He said that he understood and that there are certain things that have happened in a person's life that they would prefer to stay buried in the past and that he hopes we are able to find the answers to the questions that will help us find out what actually happened to our friend. He also warned us however, that sometimes the journey to the answers that one seeks can be filled with extremely dangerous things and one has to ask themselves if it is worth it. He shook my hand hugged me and said there is one thing that you can be sure of on your journey, that is that you should always have this man right here by your side to have your back, because that is where he has always been, and where he will always be. He then looked at Q and with a scowl on his face reached his hand out to him, shook his hand and smiled. With that Big Boy went back into the house.

As we walked away and got into the car Q said I told you we are cool and we both burst out laughing. I said man that was crazy I thought I was really going to have to shoot that fool. We then took our customary cruise down 33rd Street and hit 12th Avenue so that I could take him home. Before I dropped him off I said that it looked like things were kind of starting to come together but that I was kind of thinking about what Big Boy said about things getting dangerous and if we were willing to do what it takes to find the answers that we were seeking. I said that when this all started we asked if everyone would still be on board when it started getting a little hot, and now it appears as though that time would soon be coming. He agreed and said that he and I, Carmen and James have good lives, and that even though it is looking like two people that we were very close to were murdered under strange circumstances, we could all still go on living our lives and try to forget about the past. I said yes we could, and if that is what him, Carmen and James wanted to do I would completely understand and not hold it against them. I said it would be the smart thing for us all to do, but I just couldn't do it. I had become consumed in finding out what happened and that I was at a point where I couldn't go back to living my life without finishing what I started and finding out what happened to our friends. Q smiled and said him too, and then we shook hands and hugged before he got out of the car. Before I drove off I rolled down the window to tell him that I would get back in touch with him after I talked to Carmen to see if she had gotten any information for us. He smiled a little cat like smile and said, tell her I said hello. I looked at him with a confused look on my face, rolled the window up, and took off for home. I just wanted to kick back in my nice cool house for the rest of the day to unwind from the crazy morning that we had just had. As I drove up to the front of my house however, I realized that I was going to have to put my plans of relaxing for the day on hold for a while.

I could see that Carmen's car was parked in front of my house, and as I drove up she got out of her car to greet me. As I watched her get out of the car and uncontrollable wave of attraction took over my body, and as she walked up to me as I exited my car, my heart began to beat a little faster, and maybe because of the heat, I began to feel a little warmer and began to sweat. She said that she'd just drove up and was hoping she would catch me at home. I asked her how she was doing, and invited her in out of the heat. I was barely able to concentrate on what she said as we walked to the door, but I think it was something foobout her having found out some information for me. As we walked in I asked her to have a seat and asked her if she wanted something cold to drink. She asked what I had and I said I had water, some lemonade and some ice tea. She said she new it was a little early but she was wondering if I had any wine or a wine cooler or something. I told her I had a few wine coolers in the fridge and she said that would be fine. Normally this is something that I would be very happy about in these types of situations, because it had been my experience that if a women chose an alcoholic beverage over water or something of the non alcoholic variety, that meant she wanted to relax and get a little more comfortable, which meant there was a chance for me to move things along in a direction that would lead straight to my bedroom. This was a situation where I was hoping that wasn't the case, or, at least I think I was hoping that. I wasn't really sure what her intentions were at the time, nor was I sure what mine were. I just remember that being the longest walk ever to get that cooler, and the feeling of excitement, attraction, and guilt running through my body at the same time. This was my dead friend's girlfriend and here I was having these crazy thoughts about her that I was sure she didn't share. It had to be all in my sick and perverted head, but I couldn't help it, and I wasn't sure what I would do if she did in fact want a wine cooler to help her relax and feel free to let herself go. As I walked back with her wine cooler I could see that she had made herself comfortable on the loveseat that I had in my living room. Why did she have to sit there? Why didn't she just sit on of the more comfortable chairs that I had, or on the big comfortable couch? She'd taken her shoes off and was sitting semi Indian style with one leg folded under her and the other dangling towards the floor. I tried my best not to look but with the short, tight, white shorts she had on, I couldn't help noticing her beautiful smooth and shiny legs, and her perfect feet. Oh no, not the feet! I handed her the drink, she thanked me, and then I sat on the couch across from her, but at the end that was not directly across from her so that I could concentrate and stay focused on our conversation and not be caught looking where I shouldn't be. I asked her about her family, she asked about mine, and I slowly began to relax and come back to reality and why she had come to see me in the first place. She got very excited when I asked her what she had for me and once she began to tell me what she found, I could understand her excitement.

She began by telling me that for the past month she'd been dating a guy who worked in Internal Affairs with the Sacramento Police Department. She kind of caught me off guard by saying this and it must have shown on my face because there was an awkward pause for a moment, and she asked me what was wrong. I, pretending not to know what she was talking about said nothing, why? She responded saying that I had a kind of confused and weird look on my face when she told me she was seeing someone, and she was just wondering why. I said really, and said again that nothing was wrong, and then asked her to continue. She said that in conversations that she'd had with him, she was able to find out more information about the night that Corey was killed, and more information about the police Department's investigation into the case, and on one particular officer's involvement in not only Cory's murder, but in the death of a teenager named Raymond Brewer, and on the Oak Park Four case. At that point, she definitely had my attention, and she went on to tell me the details of what she had found out. From what she told me it seemed as though we were on the right track in looking into Michael O'Sullivan as someone who might have something to do with both Corey and Caesar's murders. She said that Michael's father Pete O'Sullivan, a racist police officer who was on the force back in the 60s and 70s and who served on the force for over 25 years. At that time, it was suspected that he, along with some of his fellow officers were members of a secret racist organization that was based out of Elk Grove, and that the group was made up of around 200 members including police officers, politicians, and pretty well connected people in the Elk Grove area at the time. The group called itself the Knights Of Liberty, and it dedicated itself to protecting the public citizens, or white Americans, from what they considered a serious threat to their safety, the Black Panther Party. Though their existence was not widely known, it was known by the Sacramento Police Department, but their activities were ignored despite many complaints that were made by the black community of being continuously harassed and terrorized by them as they drove around the black neighborhoods in the Sacramento area stopping and harassing anyone who they felt fit the description of a Black Panther member. This included basically any young black male who they wanted to stop and harass. The group was suspected of being involved in the incidents in which several Black Panther offices were fired upon, but at the time, due to the relationship between the Panthers and the SPD, there was not very much effort put into investigating the incidents let alone convicting anyone for the crimes, and they were allowed to operate their racist activities without much consequence. She then said that two weeks before Pete O'Sullivan was to retire, he was shot and killed one night while on patrol in Oak Park in an unsolved case in which he was shot in the head by sniper fire. A murder in which the original suspects were four men with known affiliations to the Black panther Party, Big Boy Patterson, Harold Brewer, Daryl Ridgeway and Terry Jenkins, the Oak Park four, the case that Big Boy had been telling us about. She confirmed that O'Sullivan was the policeman they'd had several run-ins with.

This was all slowly starting to come together and make sense. As she continued to talk I noticed that Carmen had begun to make herself a little more comfortable and begun to inch a little closer to the end of the couch where I was sitting. By this time she was sitting with her legs crossed and I had a full view of her smooth and silky legs making it impossible for me to concentrate any longer on what we were talking about. Luckily she'd pretty much finished telling me what she'd come to tell me, so I told her that I needed to go somewhere soon so it might be a good idea to wrap things up, even though I really didn't have any plans to do anything. I thanked her for the information and told her she had done a great job and gotten some very useful information that would be very helpful to us moving forward. I brought her up to date on everything else that we'd found out, and she expressed that although she had her doubts at first she really thought we were going to be able to find out what actually happened to both Corey and her brother. She then hugged me and looked into my eyes in a way that I'd seen many times before and knew what it meant. She then said she really appreciated what I was doing and if there was anything else that she could do for me or to help, that I should not hesitate to ask her. She smelled and felt so good, and as we stood there hugging each other tightly, she made a point to emphasize the word anything again, as she looked at me in a way that made me feel both excited, ashamed, and uneasy all at the same time. As she stood there seemingly waiting for me to respond, a major struggle began to take place deep inside of me between what I wanted to say and do, and what I should say and do. I smiled, looked into her beautiful eyes and said, I definitely will. I then loosened my grip on her and asked her if she wanted me to walk her to the car. A slight look of surprise and disappointment came over her face and she said thank you, yes that would be nice. We walked out of the front door and as we got closer to the car, another struggle of sorts began to come over me. One of being proud and relieved that I was able to maintain myself and not let the situation inside go any further, and one of fear and shame as I realized that I was actually very attracted to her and no matter how much I try to hide or fight it, there may come a time when I can no longer fight the feelings that I have. For now, I opened her door for her, hugged her again, told her I would be contacting her soon, and watched her drive away as I waved goodbye. I went back in the house, made me a good stiff Myers and coke, and kicked back watching something on TV for the rest of the evening. I don't even remember what it was, maybe reruns of the Twilight Zone or Night Gallery or something. I always watch stuff like that.

It now looked like Corey's death had to do with a revenge killing, and that the killers were somehow connected to Pete and Michael O'Sullivan and the racist organization that they were somehow tied to. But why Corey, and why would they need to kill Caesar also? We were so close at that point and I felt that all we needed to do was to tie a few little pieces together to solve the case.

UNWELCOME VISITORS

Mondays are always the longest day of the week for me. Don't get me wrong, I love my job and I get along with the people I work with for the most part, but after the weekend comes to an end, it is just a little hard for me to get rolling and to start the work week off. It was especially hard at that time because of everything that I was doing on the weekends to solve the case that we were working on. This particular Monday was going to be a very intriguing and little different however because I had an appointment with a couple that was having some very unusual issues with their relationship.

They weren't married yet, but were considering doing so and wanted to try and get some counseling with their relationship before they took their vows in hopes that it would help them with any issues they currently have, and hopefully, to help them avoid any they may have after they get married. This was pretty smart and progressive of them you would think, but in talking to both of them individually, there was much more to their situation than they were both willing to admit when I saw them together, when I saw them individually.

His name was Stanley Wright, and for him, there was a great fear of the commitment of being in an exclusive relationship with the same person for the rest of his life. He had always grown tired of the relationships he had been in the past after a while, usually around 4 or 5 months, and he would start feeling suffocated and wanting to get out and to find something new, fresh and exciting. He'd been with his current girlfriend Nora for a year now and had not gotten the feeling of being tied down and wanting to get out with her yet, and as a matter of fact he'd grown even closer to her over the year, closer than he'd ever been or felt for any women he'd been with before. This made him feel that maybe this was the one for him and so he proposed marriage to her and she accepted. Now, however, even though he is completely in love with her and feels that his love is growing stronger every day, he is afraid that somewhere down the line that love that he is feeling will be replaced by that old feeling of being trapped, and not ever again being able to feel the excitement and pleasure of being with someone fresh and new. It wasn't just the sex for him, although that was a huge part of it. He loved meeting and getting to know different women of all shapes, ages and races and had an almost uncontrollable desire and attraction to all of them for different reasons. He also got great excitement and pleasure out of meeting, getting to know, and eventually being intimate with all of them. He'd had many one night stands, but he preferred to be involved over a short period of time with women he met. He didn't treat them badly, and he was totally up front with all of them about who he was, and how he was, and after they realized that he was who he said he was and that their relationship would probably not be going anywhere, he would always become friends with them, friends with benefits. Although he felt he had never done anything wrong because he felt that he'd been honest with them and let them know where he was coming from the start, he always knew in the back of his minds that most of them women really liked or even loved him, and hoped that they could change him, and he felt bad and knew that they were probably hurt that it didn't happen. He felt really bad about that sometimes, but not bad enough to stop, and he would always justify his actions by telling himself that he was always honest with them, and they knew what they were getting into with him. This always made him feel better, but not much.

Her name was Nora Simpson, and she was at the other end of the spectrum. She had been in a long term relationship for five years before she met him, and she had now been with him for a year. She always liked the comfort of being in a monogamous relationship and had never wanted to stray or gotten to a point where she felt trapped. She however had a deep fear of being cheated on, because her father had constantly cheated on her mother, and her sister's marriage ended because of cheating, and her five year relationship with someone who she thought was the man of her dreams, ended because of cheating. The man who she'd loved and who she had committed and dedicated herself totally to had deceived her and cheated on her with someone who she considered one of her closest friends, creating a deep wound in her heart that eventually healed somewhat, but remained as a permanent scar that would affect any relationship with men that she would have for the rest of her life. Because of this, and to protect herself from the pain that she felt, she accepted the marriage proposal from her current fiancé, but what she hasn't told him, and planned on telling him today, is that the only condition that she has for their marriage will be for them to have an open relationship. She feels that in doing this, she could be with the person that she loves, and she did love him deeply, and she could protect herself from the hurt that she'd gotten in her previous relationship because, there wouldn't be expectation of fidelity from either of them. She felt this would give her control of the situation because when it happened it wouldn't hurt her because she would know and expect that it would happen. She just didn't want to know when, how, or with whom, and the same would be true with her if she ever decided to do it. She felt this would be the only way their relationship would work. She was wrong of course. This type of relationship would never work for either of them because it only works for people who are both completely void of jealousy, who are afraid of commitment and who therefore can love someone but still be too afraid to commit to them, who really and truly love and are completely comfortable with that type of lifestyle, and who have no desire to be in a monogamous relationship, none of which she was, and most of which he wasn't either. It was a very sticky and yet intriguing case, not just because both of them wanted to have an open relationship, but because they both wanted it for different reasons, and because neither of them knew that the other wanted it.

I'd met with both Stanley and Nora separately on several occasions prior to this, and this would be my first time meeting with them together. They showed up at my office at around 1:00 p.m.. When they came in they were holding hands and looking like a couple that was completely in love with one another and didn't have a problem in the world. They both sat down in the chairs on the other side of my desk, continuing to hold hands after they sat down. Since this would be the first time that I would be talking to them together, I would just have a preliminary discussion with them about what they both wanted out of our sessions, and then coming up with a plan and laying down ground rules for future sessions, should they want to continue coming in.

Prior to the session that day I'd asked them both before if they wanted me to be the one who broached the subject of them wanting to have an open relationship. They both responded yes. As they sat there holding hands waiting for me to start talking, I assumed that the holding of hands was a show their sign of commitment to one another, and to ease the shock of what I was going to tell the other party. I began by telling each of them that in my sessions with each of them I found that they really were in love with each other, and that they genuinely cared and wanted nothing more than to be married to each other and to make the other person happy.

While I spoke, I could tell that each of them was preparing for what I was going to tell the other, and both had a look on their faces of both concern and fear of what the other would say and do once they heard what I had to say. Before I did however, I asked both of them to tell the other how they felt about them. They both told the other how much they loved them, how much they loved being with them and spending time with them, and how much they were looking forward to their future together. Once they finished, I then let them both know that the other person wanted for their relationship to be an open one. Once I said that, they both immediately stopped holding hands, looked at each other with both a shocked and disappointed look on their face, and turned away from each other looking as if they were both crushed at what I'd just said. It was very interesting behavior, but it was also very predictable.

I then told both of them that I was a little surprised by their reaction to what I'd said since it is what they'd both said they wanted, and I said I would like both of them to tell me why they reacted the way that they did. Neither of them said a word, either because they were too angry to talk at that time, or, because they really didn't know the answer to my question. I then told them that I wanted to set up another appointment with them if they wanted to come back, and that I wanted them to think about what their answer is to my question, to share it with us the next time they were there, and along with their answer, share the reason that thought they wanted to have an open relationship in the first place. I then told them that it was my opinion that neither of them really wanted to have an open relationship because they both expressed to me that they wanted a long term relationship with each other, and that long term relationships are built on love, respect, and trust.

I went on to tell them that although people involved in open relationships can truly love one another, their main desire is the excitement of being with different people, and they don't want to be in a committed relationship. I then said that when people like them become involved in that lifestyle because of fear of being hurt, or fear of hurting someone else, or, because they don't trust others, it never works out in the long run, and they usually find that in the end those fears and trust issues are still there. I then asked both of them to give me a call to let me know if they wanted to come back, and if both of them did, I would schedule an appointment for them. They both stood up, not looking so happy at this point, shook my hand and walked out of the office, never looking at or acknowledging one another. This was going to be a very interesting case, and I couldn't wait for our next session as I was sure they both would be calling to let me know they wanted to come back. I was pretty sure anyway, maybe around 80% sure.

After my crazy and yet intriguing day at work I was dog tired and headed home for the day at around 7:00 p.m.. My plan was to call to see if James had found out any more information on Michael O'Sullivan for us. As I drove up to my house I saw an unfamiliar car parked in front of my neighbor's house. There was no-one in it so I figured the neighbors must have had some guest over or something and didn't think much more of it. As I walked in my front door I got the strangest feeling that someone had been there before I arrived. Nothing looked out of place but my bedroom door was closed and I never closed it. Something just felt off but I just couldn't place my finger on what it was. I went to the kitchen and grabbed a Pepsi out of the refrigerator. I got a glass out of the cabinet, filled it with ice, and pored the Pepsi in it. As I walked back into the living room I picked up the phone to call James but as I started to dial the numbers, I looked up towards my bedroom and noticed that the door to my room was now open. Just as I put the phone down to go and see what the hell was going on, I felt a sharp pain in the back of my head and everything went black. I was knocked out cold.

When I came to everything was a little blurry and I had a throbbing pain in my head. I was sitting in the chair in my living room facing three guys standing in front of me who looked like either low life thugs or plain clothes police officers, I couldn't tell which at the time. I normally would be able to easily distinguish between the two, but my head was still a little fuzzy and I couldn't tell what they were. I guess at the time it didn't really matter. What did matter was they were in my house and I hadn't invited them, and they'd hit me over the head and tied me to a chair. As I struggled to regain my faculties and clear my head, they all just stood there looking at me for a moment. Suddenly, the smaller of the three, noticing that I had awakened, said that he heard that I'd been asking questions about Michael O'Sullivan.

I didn't respond, so the biggest of the three punched me in my gut so hard it completely knocked all of the wind out of me, and I almost passed out again. I asked who they were and the guy who was doing all of the talking said never mind who they were, and that he was not making a statement when he asked me what he'd asked me, he was asking a question, and if I didn't want his two friends to get upset and to beat the shit out of my black ass, I'd better answer. He then repeated his question, a little louder this time. I said yes, I'd been asking questions about O'Sullivan. He then asked me why, and again I didn't answer. This time the other guy, who'd just been standing there up to this point, slapped me so hard across the face that I could tell my nose started to bleed. He then punched me in the nuts and I doubled over in pain. The smaller guy then grabbed me tightly by my shirt, and again asked why I'd been asking questions about Michael O'Sullivan? Again, I didn't say anything, I couldn't. If I lied, they could easily find out that I was lying. If I told the truth, it would put people who I loved and cared about in danger, if they weren't already. I would just have to keep my mouth shut and take this ass whooping, if that was all it was going to be. Hopefully it wouldn't get any worse than that. They all took turns punching and slapping me around a bit, not enough where I would need medical attention, but enough where I could get the idea that they were serious.

Just then, Q and Big Boy busted in the door and before the three intruders had a chance to say anything, Big Boy laid all three of them out with three straight punches. At least I think it was three. It happened so fast I couldn't really tell. I do remember hearing 3 distinct punches that sounded like someone hitting a slab of meat with a sledgehammer, and the next thing I knew all three of the men were laid out on the floor in front of me, knocked out cold. They quickly untied me , we picked the three of them up, and after a brief disagreement on whose car to use to take them and dump them somewhere, we put them in the trunk of Face's car, quickly drove them over to Curtis park, and dropped them by the side of the curb. We then headed back to my house.

On the way we were all trying to figure out who these guys were. I said I had planned to call James when I first got home and Big Boy reiterated that he didn't know why I trusted James and said that he was a cop and they always watched out for each other no matter what. He said it is that blue shield mentality that they had and that they all bleed PD blue blood. Q agreed with him and I must say, even though deep down inside my gut I still trusted James, I did have some questions that I would be asking him once he came by that evening. How had these guys found out that I was asking questions about O'Sullivan? Had James told them? That would be the only way they would have known. There was only one way to find out. I had to call him.

I had the guys drop me off and told them to come back by the house in about an hour. I told them I would be having James and Carmen come by so that we could talk about what happened and to find out if either of them found out any more information that we could use. Once inside I quickly went to check myself out in the bathroom mirror to see the extent of the damage that had been done to my face. It wasn't bad, the beginnings of a black eye and the remnants of a bloody nose, but overall I was still my beautifully handsome self. I would be feeling the beating that I had been given to my body for a few days though, and my nuts would also be hurting for a while. I went into the living room and did what I'd started to do earlier before I'd been detained by my unwelcome guest, called James. When he answered I said his name, and once he heard that it was me, he quickly responded, his voice sounding both irritated and relieved at the same time. He asked where I'd been, and that he'd tried to call me earlier and it seemed like I answered the phone but when he'd said my name a few times it hung up. I asked him when he called, and he said about an hour ago, which was around the time that I'd been knocked unconscious. I asked him if he'd heard anything when it sounded like the phone had been answered, and he said he could hear someone breathing and he thought it was me. He said he said hello a few times but that there was no answer.

I asked him to think very carefully about what I was going to ask him because it was very important. I asked if at any time during the call he had said his name. He thought for a moment and said he didn't think so. I said it is very important that he knew for sure, and to think very hard to try to remember if he said his name during the call. He though for a few seconds more and then said that he did say his name right before he hung up, and that he said, it was J dog and to call him back as soon as possible. I asked if he was sure he said J Dog and not James and he said he was sure. I then proceeded to tell him what happened, and that I was sure it was cops who had paid me a visit.

After I finished telling him what happened, he asked if I was sure I was ok, and that he was going to come by to tell me some stuff that he had found out, and that might explain why I had gotten visitors. It was already around 9:00 p.m. and close to my bedtime during the work week, I was very tired and worn out from the long work day and of course by what had happened , and I didn't really know whether to trust him or not at that time, but I needed to know what he had to tell me, and my instinct told me that I could still trust him, so I told him to come on by and I was glad that I did, because what he had to tell us made it all start to make sense, and brings more in focus and in line as to what really happened to our friends, and why.

PATH TO DARKNESS

James arrived at my house at around 10:00 p.m. and Q and Carmen showed up about 10 -15 minutes later. Big Boy hadn't shown up yet but he was always late. I figured he decided to take a pass because he still didn't quite trust James, which was cool. It was a little late but I was still kind of hyped, partly in anticipation of what James had to tell us, and partly from the adrenalin rush I still had from being worked over by those punks. Either way, I wasn't tired anymore. Carmen and James were concerned by my appearance but after assuring them all that I would be ok, James proceeded to tell us what he'd found out.

He began by saying that the deaths of Corey, Caesar and Raymond Brewer were all connected in some way or another, and that they all involved Michael O'Sullivan, his father Pete, and the secret organization that the older O'Sullivan helped to form back in the early 70s. The organization was called the Knights of Liberty and he continued on by saying that he'd talked to a couple of retired officers who worked in the Department back at that time, and they told him that the organization was originally formed by several officers who were on the force at the time to as they put it, protect the country, or more specifically, the white race, from black militant organizations such as the Black Panthers.

The organizers of the KOL felt that the Panthers, who J. Edgar Hoover felt was the greatest threat to the U. S. Security at the time, were a danger to all white Americans and these feelings were cultivated and perpetuated by the KOL, and in particular its leader Pete O'Sullivan. The organization was supported by other racist organizations at the time because of the propaganda and misinformation that was put out. The organizers fed into this paranoia, and said that they created their organization or club as they called it, to protect the white community from not only the Panthers, but from any group that they felt threatened white people and their rights as white Americans. In other words they, they considered themselves as the white version of the Black Panthers, using what hey felt was the same philosophy or similar reason for their creation as the Panthers used for theirs. Eventually however, as it always does with organizations that are formed based on racist ideas and ideologies, KOL turned into a full fledged racist organization, which was run by racist police officers led by Pete O'Sullivan.

James continued by saying that in order to accomplish their mission and to get rid of the Panthers, the officers would take any opportunity that they could while they were on patrol or off duty, to harass, assault, and attempt to intimidate any black person or persons they felt fit the description of potentially being involved with the Black Panther party. They also harassed anyone else who wasn't what they considered to be true and pure Americans, which included Hispanics, Asians, and basically anyone who wasn't white. Their main focus and obsession was the Panthers however, and they harassed young black men on a daily basis, most of the time without provocation. James said that although the KOL was supposedly being watched by the FBI and by local Law enforcement, their existence, which was pretty much known by everyone at the time, was ignored, and the reports of incidents involving their harassment of young black men were also either ignored, or quickly written off as justified and swept under the rug. They basically had a license to harass anyone, anywhere, and at anytime they wanted.

I then told James that I understood what he was telling us so far, and that what he was describing to us we pretty much already knew, and what we needed to know was how it related to the deaths of Cory, Caesar and Raymond.

He went on to tell us about the incident that Pete O'Sullivan and some of his fellow officers were involved in back in 1973 in which they rousted a Black Panthers headquarter and were accused of shooting several people including children. He said that they were brought up on charges, but the charges were dropped, the shootings were found to be justified, and they were placed back on duty. This had to be the same incident that our friend

Big Boy had described to us and it confirmed that what he'd told us was true. It also confirms that Pete O'Sullivan was the was also the officer that had gotten shot and killed by sniper fire, a murder that Big Boy and his friends, the Oak Park Four, had been accused and charged with, but were found innocent of committing. It all fit together.

James continued by saying that several years after his father's murder, Michael O'Sullivan also joined the force and specifically asked to be assigned to the Oak Park area. James said that he'd gone to the academy with Michael, and that they'd both graduated at the top of their class, but that he said he always felt that O'Sullivan had a huge chip on his shoulder and had a hidden agenda or a different goal or path that he'd set out on when joining the force, a 'path to a dark place' as he put it. He said that Michael had always gotten along with all of the other cadets while at the academy, but that he had an obvious dislike hatred for the non white cadets, and that this dislike continued when they both were assigned to the same precinct that patrolled the Oak Park area. Something else that he said that was very interesting was that he'd had a conversation with O' Sullivan when they first were assigned to the Oak Park beat in which he half jokingly asked him if he was ready to serve and protect. He said O'Sullivan looked at him with a very serious and almost evil look in his eye and responded, no, I am ready to get some payback. He said at the time he didn't think much of it, and just wrote off O'Sullivan as being just another racist cop, but based on some other things that he found out, he thought that O'Sullivan was definitely a person of interest for us.

He then went on to tell us that there was a boy who'd been shot and killed by two plain clothes police officers who were on patrol and looking for some guys who'd been pulling armed robberies at stores in the Oak Park area back in 1979. He said that the two officers' stories were that they accidentally shot the teenager after stopping him and his friends, thinking they fit the description of the robbery suspects. They'd said that after stopping the teens, the boys took off running, and after giving chase, they shot one of them, killing him. He said that one of the officers who'd been involved in the shooting was O'Sullivan and that after an investigation, it was determined that the shooting was an accident and justified. I asked if he knew the teenagers name and he said it was Marcello, the boy who'd been shot the year before Corey. I began to get chills after hearing this. I still didn't know however, how these two things related to Corey and Caesar's deaths and I asked James how they did. He said that he could see why I would wonder that, but that after he told me what he was going to tell me next, we would all see how these two things were connected to both Corey and Caesar's deaths. We all listened very closely like we were listening to someone tell spooky stories around a campfire.

He continued on to say that on the night that Corey was murdered, he had gotten a call on his radio asking for all officers in the area of the shooting to go to the scene, and that he and his partner were the second car to arrive. Once they got there, Caesar was sitting on the side of the curb already in cuffs, and that he kept saying he's dead, he's dead, and that he placed him in the back of his car. He said that it was about that time that Carmen came out of the house, and upon seeing Corey, began screaming and yelling uncontrollably, and seeing her brother in the back of our car, and began screaming at him that he killed him. He said that things began happening so fast at that point, and just when he went to Carmen and put his arm around her to try to comfort her, other patrol cars rolled up with their lights flashing, and lots of neighbors began coming out of their houses to see what was going on. At that time James said that he got together with the other officers and that they decided that the best thing to do at that time would be for him to take Caesar downtown for questioning and to get him away from the scene to prevent anything from escalating. He then said that on that night, there were four patrol cars assigned to the area, 3 regular cars and one undercover car, but that only the three regular cars showed up, and when he checked to see who was in the car that hadn't shown up he found out that it was O'Sullivan who'd just got back on duty after being suspended. Not only that, but when questioning the neighbors about anything that they'd seen in regards to the incident, an older lady said that she didn't see the shooting but that she heard gunfire, and when peeking out of the window, she thought she'd seen a car speeding away, but she couldn't be sure. She said that she figured it was whoever did the shooting and that she would be asked about it at some point. He said that when he saw O'Sullivan back at headquarters later, he asked him what happened to him when the call came out, and he said that he'd been having some trouble with his car, and by the time he was able to go, the call went out that everything was ok. We had a short discussion about what happened and he showed very little concern. He said he didn't really think much of it after that because it was pretty much an open and shut case that Caesar had done it.

He then looked at Carmen and said that it made him sick that he didn't do more to further look into the case, and he told her that he hoped she accepted his sincere apology, and she, crying by this time, softly said she did forgive him. He then told her that she hoped she continued to feel that way after he told us what he was going to say next. He then asked if we could guess who just happened to be in the area on the night that I'd met Caesar at the bar and the night he'd been shot and killed. We all said Michael O'Sullivan in unison as it was painfully obvious that it would be him. He then showed me a picture of O'Sullivan and asked me to think carefully if I'd seen him before. I didn't have to think too hard though. As soon as I looked at the picture I knew where I'd seen him. It was the drunken man at the end of the bar on the night that I met Caesar at The Touch. The man who we thought was harassing the woman, and the guy who Caesar had knocked out. Apparently he'd been following Caesar and was in the area on the night that he was killed.

With the information that James had given us the pieces had all fallen into place. It was starting to look like Corey and Marcello Rainwater, the boy who'd been shot and killed by police a year before Corey's death, were both killed by Michael O'Sullivan as revenge for his father being shot and killed back in the 1975 by who he believed to be the McClatchy Park 4, which included Corey's father Donald (Donnie) Jenkins and Marcello's father Joseph (Jojo) McFerrin, Big Boy Patterson and Daryl Ridgeway. We figured that by killing Corey and Marcello, the kids of two of the men he felt killed his father, Michael felt that he would be causing the men to feel the pain of loss that he felt when he lost his father. As far as Caesar was concerned, it appears as though he heard Michael's secret from the guard while in prison, and once he got out he planned to tell me so that I could help him prove it and thereby proving his innocence. Before he was able to do this however, Michael O'Sullivan found out that he knew his secret and perhaps his plans, and then killed him to keep him quiet.

After everyone left that evening I called Big Boy and told him what we'd found out. I also warned him that he might want to keep a very close eye on his daughter Korryn to make sure she is protected and stays out of harm's way. When I finished telling him what I had to say the phone was silent for a moment and then he asked if I was sure about what I was saying. I told him that I was pretty sure, but that we still needed to check out everything to confirm what James told us, but that in the meantime we shouldn't take any chances in case what he was telling us was true. There were a few more moments of silence before Big Boy spoke again, at which time he just said, hmm. I asked him what was up, and then asked him if he'd seen or talked to his daughter recently. He said that he'd just talked to her the day before and she'd said that she was going to be hanging out with friends that evening and would call him when she got home, but that she'd never called to check in with him. I asked him if that was unusual, and he said yes, because they had an agreement that he didn't care what she did or what time she got home as long as she would always call him to let her know she made it home safely, and that this was probably the first time that she didn't do that. With that, I said that he might want to call her to see what's up, but I assured him that she was probably ok and too tired to call him when she got home. He said,

"Yeah you're right,"

He then thanked me for the information and said he had to go, probably to immediately call and check on his daughter. Before he got off of the phone however, I told him that I wanted to get together with him, Q, James and Carmen to decide what our next move would be. I told him I would like to do it the next day, which was Sunday, sometime in the evening. He said that would be fine with him, and before he hung up, I told him not to worry, everything was probably ok with his daughter, but to be sure to call me to let me know she is ok after he talks to her. He said ok, and even though I hoped that what I was telling him was the truth, I had a really strange feeling inside that she could be in trouble. I hoped I was wrong.

The next day I went by Q's house to hang out and to kind of come up with a preliminary plan for moving forward that we could tell the others when we met with them later that day. When I got there he was in his driveway waxing up his car, which he did 2 to 3 times a week. Q is a different kind of guy. He always seemed to be conflicted as to whether he wants to be a deeply religious, dedicated Christian man, or a wild, partying, womanizing player, not caring about anything else but his own satisfaction. He always seemed to be at one extreme or the other, never in the middle, and that made it difficult for him to find and develop relationships with not only women, but with people in general. It has to be a lonely way to live because when you keep changing yourself and how you act, no-one really knows who you really are. I knew who he was though. He was both good and bad just like the rest of us. He just needed to realize at some point that he could be somewhere in the middle, and it would be ok. I would always ask him though, which Q I was dealing with at the time, the good one or the bad one. He would always smile, and tell me which one it was, and we would precede from there. Sometimes I wouldn't have to ask him though. For example, today he is in the driveway with his shirt off waxing his car. That meant that the bad Q was out in full force, trying to flex his skinny chest for any babes that might be going by, and shining his car up getting ready to go out on the town later in the evening. So I didn't have to ask him.

As I walked up to him I asked, "What are you doing out here with your shirt off, showing everyone that bird chest?"

He smiled, laughed, and then said, "Just shining up Betty Boop."

That is what he called his car. I told him that I called Big Boy to tell him what we'd find out and to warn him that he should keep an eye on his daughter, but that he was worried because he hadn't seen or talked to her since the morning before. I said that the reason he was worried was because he and his daughter had a deal that whenever she went out with friends at night, which she'd done the night before, she would call him to let him know that she was ok when she got home, no matter what time it was. I also said I told Big Boy that she was probably ok, but to call me as soon as he heard from her to let me know what was up. I said that even though I told him that, I was a little worried about her, especially after what James had to us. Q said, "I'm sure she is ok, she was probably just out hanging out with friends having fun like you said."

I replied, " I hope so; if not, we might have another issue on our hands" Q said, "Na, I am sure she is ok."

It was something about the way he said it that second time however that didn't seen quite right. His cool and calm demeanor when I told him she was missing, and the smile he got on his face when he said he was sure she was ok gave me an uneasy feeling and sent a chill through my bones. I asked him

"How are you so sure she's ok? Stop washing the car and look at me while I'm talking to you."

"What are you talking about?"

A big smile came across his face and he actually started to laugh. Just then, his front door opened, and out walked Korryn, Big Boy's daughter. I couldn't believe it. This was the same daughter that Big Boy had warned Corey about and the same daughter that he had told us he would kill for if he ever found out we messed with her. All I could do was to look at her, look at Q in disbelief, and then drop my head. Was this fool crazy? Was he trying to get us killed? Here we are trying to set up a meeting with Big Boy to help us solve this shit, and he is up here sleeping with the man's daughter after he said he would kill us over her. All I could do was walk to my car to leave. As I got in, Q came running up to the car to try to explain, but there was nothing he could say at that point that would make any sense to me or that could explain what I had just seen. He is either crazy or he just doesn't get it. He said, "P, she's been trying to contact me ever since her pops told her we went by there that day. I have been dodging her but she finally caught me in front of my house one day and one thing led to another, it was Big Boy's fault"

He smiled again.

I looked at him is disbelief.
"How is that? How is it his fault?"

"If he would have never told her that he talked to us, she would have never tried looking for me, and nothing would have ever happened."

I just looked at him. He looked serious, so serious in fact that it almost made me smile. He was crazy. I asked him

"Are you crazy or do you have some kind of mental condition that I don't know about?"

I was really starting to believe that he was not all there. I then looked him dead in his eyes and said, "I wanted to make something very clear to you, crystal clear in fact, you are on your own on this. I don't have your back if something jumps off with Big Boy over this, because you ain't getting me caught up over some bullshit that you could have avoided if you were thinking with your right head."

I asked him if he understood what I was telling him and to repeat what I'd just said just in case there miss some misunderstanding or miscommunication between what I said and what he heard. He repeated what I'd just said and then said that it was cool. I started my car ready to take off. I told him I would see him the next day, he said ok and turned to walk away. Before I took off however, he turned back around again and asked me to roll down the window. I turned my music down, rolled down the window and asked

"What's up?"

He looked at me, and with a serious look on his face he said,

"You really wouldn't have my back P?"

I looked back at him with a serious and yet perplexed look on my face, and didn't say a word. I just smiled, turned up the music full blast, and drove off. As I looked in the rearview mirror I could see Q still standing there, holding his stomach laughing, knowing that some questions don't ever really need to be asked because the answer is known already. Q was my boy, my best friend. I would always have his back no matter what.

JAMES COOL

When I got home I contacted everyone, Q, Carmen, James, and Big Boy, and told them to meet me at my house that evening at around 5:00. They all arrived on time, all except James who was going to be a little late because he had to have a meeting with his sergeant at 4:00 and would come by afterwards. I told him we would start without him since we would first be going over information that he already knew, and we could catch him up on anything that he missed. After the others arrived I told them that James would be late and we could start without him. To my surprise they all expressed concerns about him being involved in what we were doing. They all liked him and thought he was a pretty cool guy, but they said none of us really know him, and because he is a police officer, they didn't feel comfortable talking around him, and quite frankly they didn't trust him, especially not Big Boy, which was predictable. Big Boy didn't even trust us, let alone a white man that he didn't know. A white man that he didn't know that was also a police officer.

I told him that I understood all of them being skeptical of James, and that they all had concerns about him being involved, but assured them that I trusted him, and if they trusted me, they could also trust that I would know if he wasn't on the up and up. Of course I didn't know for sure if I was telling them the truth, but I knew that if we were going to be successful with any plan that we would come up moving forward, he would be a critical resource that we would not be able to do without. So I felt it was worth what I felt was a very small risk of having him on board. I told him that he'd already proved to me that he could trusted because he'd actually saved my life before, something that took them all by surprise, especially Q because I'd never told him before. I then went on to tell them something that I'd never told anyone before, one, because it wasn't really anyone's business and two and most importantly, it was something that happened that didn't reflect very well on me.

It all happened one evening when he and I headed over to Baxter's on Sunrise to hang out and try to pick up on some ladies. Sunrise, which is in Citrus Heights, is around 95% white, but there are several clubs over there that were pretty cool and that I was crazy enough to go check out from time to time. Plus, I was with James, a white police officer, so I didn't think I would have any issues going there. After we'd been there for a while, this beautiful white girl that was standing at the bar all alone had been checking me out from the time we walked in the door. She was gorgeous with a beautiful, slightly muscular body, beautiful long legs, and a tight mid length skirt with the long split in the side, and absolutely perfect feet, which I could also see because she had on some high heeled candies. All of the men would stop in mid sentence or turn to watch her when she passed by them. All but me that is, since I knew it was me that she wanted. Maybe she was into the brothers and I was the only one in the place, or, maybe it was just because she found me irresistible.

Whatever the reason, I could tell that she wanted me and after being there a very short time she walked up to me and James while we were at the bar drinking on our Long Islands. I was already feeling pretty good at that point, which made me feel a little braver than I normally did, so when she asked me if I wanted to dance, I said yes despite all the hard looks I got from all of the guys as we walked out to the floor. From that point on, she was all over me the rest of the evening, and at closing time, she asked me if I wanted to come with her to her house. I told her I had to talk to my man James first since I came with him, and he asked if I were sure, and said that he was a little concerned and felt kind of funny about it. He said that something didn't seem right, and that he didn't trust her for some reason, and again asked if I was sure. At that time, I remember thinking he was tripping, and that maybe he was probably jealous like all of the other white boys that was there. I told him I would be cool, and he finally said ok and that he would catch up with me later. So I got in her car with her, a brand new, red, corvette, my all time favorite car, and we took off for her house.

After around 30 minutes, I realized that we were leaving the city and heading into the hills. I asked her how far she lived and she just smiled and said that it wouldn't be much longer. After about another thirty minutes I starting tripping a little, not really worried, but a little disturbed and wondering where the hell this woman lived. At that point, she quickly took a left and started going up a hill for what seemed like fifteen to twenty minutes. I told her I was starting to trip a little because I'd never been in this area before, and that I knew it was nothing but white folks up there. I jokingly asked her if she was taking me somewhere where she had a couple of good old boys waiting to string me up or something. She laughed and said, no, what's the matter are you scared? I said no, but how much further is your place? Just then she made a quick right to turn into a driveway, turned off the car, and said we were there. She grabbed my face with both hands, gave me a long slow kiss, looked in my eyes, and asked me to follow her. So I followed her into her house. It was pitch black when she opened the door. As I went to turn the light on she stopped me, lined me up close behind her, took both of my hands, and led me to a couch that was in her living room. We sat down and she immediately pulled me on top of her and we began kissing wildly and pulling at each others clothes. Just when I thought we were getting ready to make it happen, the lights came on. As we looked at each other, she had a shocked look on her face at first, but after a second or two her shock look turned into a smile.

She pushed me up off of her and looking towards the dark she said, " It's about time, I was starting to think you wasn't going to show up, I was almost hoping you would be a little late."

I was totally confused. Was she talking to me? As I looked up a cold and helpless feeling took over me as looked over and saw who she was talking to. Four huge white boys with skinned heads, white t shirts and what liked like army boots were standing on the other side of the room. They were skinheads. I hadn't encountered them before, but I'd heard stories about them and what they did to the brothas when they ran across them or when they caught them alone. This wasn't good, not good at all. I was in a situation where I could lose my life or get messed up really badly, and I had no idea where I was. I was somewhere in the mountains, out in the wilderness, no car, and no one knew where I was. James was the last person that I'd talked to that I knew that evening and I pretty much told him to get lost and that I didn't need him. Well, I couldn't have been more wrong because this bitch got me up here in a situation where I was completely vulnerable and the only way that I was going to get out was to try to fight may way out, take her car, and try to find my way back to the freeway so that I could go home. Given the circumstances however, this was going to be a very difficult if not impossible thing to do. I could probably handle the situation if it were only a couple of them, but these were four big redneck muthafuckers, who had the look in their eyes like they were looking a an animal that they were about to slaughter. I was going to my assed kicked, or maybe even killed, there was no way around it.

After a few moments of laughing, one of them shouted at me

"What the fuck are you doing with my woman boy?"

I got up, looked at him, looked at her, and then looked back at him and said, "I didn't know she was your woman, she was the one who picked me up and brought me here."

"If I knew she was with someone, I wouldn't have come up here with her."

"I am not looking for any trouble, and I would appreciate it if y'all would just let me go on my way."

They all broke out in laughter at this of course, including the girl. The guy then asked her

"Is that true babe, did you pick him up and bring him here?"

She looked at me and said, "Of course, ain't that what you asked me to do, go to the club, pick up on a black buck, and bring him back here so you guys could have some fun with him?"

He said, "Yeah, that is right, that is what I asked you to do. It works every time don't it? These monkeys just can't resist it when a pretty young white girl acts like they want to get with them."

 He then directed his attention to me and said,

"Can you?"

I didn't say anything, and it seemed to piss him off and he started to walk towards me and in a louder voice said,

"I am talking to you fucking nigger, I said you monkeys can't resist a pretty little girl like this can you?"

This time I felt compelled to answer him and I said

"No, I guess not"

They all started laughing again. Suddenly, and without thinking and acting basically on instincts, I grabbed the girl and got her in a headlock. All of the rednecks, who had started creep towards me by this time, stopped in their tracks and I said

"I'll break this bitch's neck if any of you muthafuckas get any closer"
I'd gotten myself a few extra seconds to think up some way of getting out of this situation, but my brief moment of reprieve was short lived as the one skinhead, who must have been the leader said to the other three,

"I guess she will just be a casualty of war, grab his black ass so we can skin him alive."

These fools were crazy, I was going to have to take my chances and try to fight my way past all four of them as best as I could. If I got taken out, I was going to take as many of them with me as I could. I remember thinking I couldn't believe that I'd gotten my arrogant ass in that situation, and if I'd listened to James I wouldn't be where I was, and thinking my family and my friends, and all kinds of shit that people think of when think they might be getting ready to die. At that point the woman hit me in the nuts as hard as she could and although I didn't let her go, it hurt and stunned me so much that it gave the rednecks a chance to grab me from behind and to free her from my grasp. I was able to shake myself free, and as they tried to grab me again I punched one of them in the jaw as hard as I could and I think I knocked him out cold. The other two that had grabbed me however, were able to grab me again, this time with a firmer grip, and the fourth one, who'd been standing by up to this point, kneed me in the nuts again, and I doubled over on to the floor. They then all started to kick me with their steel toed boots, but while lying there, I was able to grab one of them by the leg when he tried to kick me and I wrestled him to the floor, got on top of him, and started punching him in the face as hard as I could, until I felt him go limp. Just then I felt a sharp pain as something struck me in the back of the head almost knocking me out. As I fell to the floor I could see that one of the two remaining rednecks had hit me with the butt of his handgun. Just then I heard a loud bang and the sound of what sounded like a door crashing open. As I looked at the front door, half dazed from the blow to my head, I saw that it was James standing there with a sawed off shotgun in his hands. Not trusting the woman and following his gut, he'd followed behind us at a distance so as not to alarm us that we were being followed, but far enough that we did not notice him. He'd caught the two skinheads totally by surprise. He yelled, "I am a police officer, get the fuck back and put your hands over your heads!"

Partly because they were surprised, and partly because they were stupid, they didn't listen to him at first, so he said, "I am only going to repeat myself one time, and one time only, and then Ima start blasting you redneck muthafuckas, starting with the bitch."

This time I think they believed him, so they all, including the woman, put their hands over their heads. He then asked the woman where the phone was and to bring it to him, which she did. As she handed it to him however, the one who'd acted like the leader, thinking this would be his only chance, reached down to grab the gun that he'd dropped, in an attempt to grab it and to shoot James. It was a very foolish calculation on his part because just as he grabbed it James unloaded on him, blasting him in his shoulder and knocking him to the floor, screaming in agony. Hearing him scream, James coldly told him, "You're lucky, I could have blown your head off instead of just wounding you."

He then went ahead and called the police to come out to the scene. We didn't have any problem with the other three until the police cars arrived on the scene. While we were waiting for them I asked James what had made him decide to follow me, and what took him so long to come in? He said that he'd told me that he didn't trust that woman, but I wasn't hearing him because I was letting my other head do the thinking for me at that time, so he just decided to follow us to make sure everything was ok. He said that he took so long to come in because we'd actually lost him on one of the winding roads we took and that he was just getting ready to just go back to the freeway when he ran across the car that we'd been in, in the driveway. He said that I was lucky that he'd seen the car, because he was definitely on his way back to the freeway and home when he saw the car by accident. I thanked him and told him that he saved my life, and he said, no problem, that is what friends are for, and that he just hoped I would do the same for him if he were in that situation one day, and I told him that I definitely would, and that I owed him.

So that is why I consider James a real friend, why I trust him, and asked him to help us to solve this case. After I finished telling them my story they all felt better about trusting James and agreed that he should be involved in what we were doing. All except Big Boy of course, but like I said, he didn't even trust us so it was cool. As long as he did what he needed to do and didn't stop us or James from doing what we needed to do it would be ok.

JAMES GETS IN

When James arrived at my house at around 7:00 p.m., we began to trying to devise a plan that would not only give us an air tight case against O'Sullivan and put him in prison for the rest of his life, it would also destroy to KOL, the racist organization that his father had created and that he kept going after his father's death. Finally, and most importantly to us, it would also completely exonerate Caesar of Corey's murder and allow both him and Corey to rest in peace.

We started by going over the different scenarios and weighing the pros and cons of each in hopes that the most obvious and effective solution would jump out as the path that we should take. We sat for hours going over each one plan very carefully, over and over and over again. Then, after 5 hours of heated discussion going back and forth over the best path to take, we finally came to the conclusion that none of them were full proof, all of them would be dangerous and even life threatening for all of us, and the only thing that we could do would be to try and choose the one that was probably the most dangerous and risky, but that would expose the truth completely, and without any question or doubt of who was responsible for the murders. We decided not to contact the authorities to help us because we didn't how many people who worked with the O'Sullivans' that might be involved.

We decided that the plan would be for James to try to get close to O'Sullivan and join his organization. Once he got in, he would try to find out as much as he could about what the organization's purpose was, any illegal activities they were involved in, and if possible, find out if O'Sullivan was involved in the murders of Corey and Caesar. He would need to find any evidence that he could that would be rock solid enough for us to use to convict him and or break up his organization for good. James was more than willing to do this not just because he wanted to help us, which was reason enough for him, but for his own selfish reasons. Let's be real, when someone becomes a police officer they are handed a great deal of power, the power that comes from wearing a police uniform, wearing a badge, carrying a gun, and having the authority to enforce their will over others just because of who they are and what they do for a living. There is a saying that with great power comes great responsibility and that is very true when it comes to being an officer of the law. The thing is, people fall on two sides of the fence when it come to their view of police officers as a whole, those who respect and honor those who wear a badge, and who appreciate everything that officers do and sacrifice in performing their duties, and those who fear, dislike and don't trust those who wear a badge. The side of the fence you are on can be determined by many factors including the color of your skin, your dealings with them, good, or bad, how you grew up, where you grew up, and lastly and most importantly, how you have been treated when you have had interactions with them.

Police officers are human just like everyone else, which means they can be single, married, have kids, not have kids, they can be white, black, Hispanic, Asian, or any other race. They can have good days, bad days, up days and down days. They can be sensitive or they can be hard. They can be really good people, bad people, racially sensitive to people of all races, religions or economic backgrounds, or, they can be racist and hateful towards everyone but their own race or, those who believe as they do. The scary thing is, when you get police officers that have been given the power that they all have, who are hateful, racist, and criminals, who hide behind their badges to commit crimes against other people, it is a huge problem.

James had a deep seated dislike and hatred for police officers who were crooked, corrupt, or who abused their power and authority as officers of the law, His hatred goes way back to when he was a young man growing up in New York City. His father was also a police officer and he worked in what was considered the dirtiest precinct in the city at the time the 75th precinct. Although he was squeaky clean James told me that he remembers his father always coming home and complaining about the other cops who were dirty and on the take, and how they were a disgrace to their badges and uniforms. He would say that they would always approach to go along with what they were doing, and when he didn't he was ostracized because they felt they couldn't trust him. James said he remembers a particular time when Sony O' Rourke, who was probably the dirtiest cop in New York, asked his father to go along with him on a job to stake down one of the biggest drug dealers in New York. He said that times were really tough for their family at that time because his younger brother was very sick and in need of medical care that they just couldn't afford at that time, and his father feeling the pressure from his buddies to go along, and his brother's skyrocketing medical bills, decided that he would finally do it. He said that he can remember his father leaving the house that might and telling his mother that everything would be ok, but if something were to happen, to pack up the kids and to go and stay with his grandmother for a while until he could straighten things out. He said he then told her he loved her and left the house, leaving her crying and sitting on the couch. He said that he was around 13 at the time, and he went to his mother and asked her what was wrong, and she smiled at him and told him that everything was fine. He said he then asked where his father had gone, and she said that he'd gone to do a little extra work to get some money to pay for his brother to get well. He then said that she then, probably sensing that he was a little confused and worried by what was going one, gently place both of her hands on his cheeks and said to always remember that she and his dad loved them very much, and that they would always do anything to make sure that they are have everything that they need, and that they are always safe. He then said that she told him to go to his room. After an hour went by, his father came back home, and he could hear his mom ask him what happened, to which he replied that he couldn't do it. He then began to cry, apologized to her saying that he was sorry, but that he just couldn't do it. She hugged him, told him that it was ok and that they would figure something out, and not to worry.

Later that month, there was a huge crackdown on corruption in the precinct, and many of the officers that his dad had worked with for many years, were arrested, charged, and sent to prison. The only ones that weren't were himself and a small number of officers who never got caught up in the things that the other officers had been into. Some of the officers who had gotten caught up, and who had been arrested, accused James's father and the other cops of being rats and telling on them. It wasn't true though. Even though he was never involved in what was going on, he would never have told on his fellow officers, or his brothers as he called it, and he didn't even when he was called to testify against them.

He had a blind loyalty to them no matter how crooked or terrible the things were that they did. This would eat away at him for years however, causing him to drink heavily, get strung out on heroine for a period of time, and cause problems in the marriage to his mother that would cause them to divorce after 30 years of marriage.

When James entered the academy, his father sat him down and told him the story of what happened to him and how he didn't come forward to tell what he knew about his fellow officers who he knew were doing terrible things. He said that not telling on them allowed many good people to suffer as a result of the things that they were doing, and by him knowing and not doing the right thing and telling on them, he himself was partly responsible. He said that this had a huge impact on him, his life, and his career and on his personal life and if he had the chance to go back and do it all over again, he would have come forward and told, regardless of the consequences as a result of it. He then told James something that he would never forget, that whatever he did in life and as an officer of the law, to never let the blue shield blind him to his responsibilities as an human being and as an officer of the law, and that that wasn't to go along with the idea of being part of a blue shield that always came first no matter what, but that is main obligation and duty was to protect and serve the public, and that if he couldn't do that, he should stop right then and not go down the path he was getting ready to take.

Unfortunately James's father passed away right before he graduated from the academy , but what he told James that day stuck with him, and he lives his father's words to this day.

James knew that the quickest way that he could get in with Michael would be to gain his trust. How could he do this though? He didn't want to break any laws or commit a criminal act to do it because that would make him no better than him. It could also land him in trouble since he wasn't officially working undercover. He would have to make O'Sullivan come to him. Because he already knew him, and had already talked to and established a cordial relationship with him, hopefully, it wouldn't take much time for him to gain his trust and to be recruited into his group. Although there were already quite a few people involved, Michael was very ambitious and eager to gain as many members as he could and to do it as quickly as possible, he new that with this type of hate group there could only be strength in numbers. And that is what his main focus was, and what would also make it easier for James to get in. While he was doing this he would not be able to have very much contact with us and we would have to be extremely careful when we did meet with him so that his cover wouldn't be blown, putting him in extreme danger and potentially ruining any chance we had of solving our case and our goal to put O'Sullivan behind bars and breaking up his and his father's racist organization for good. He began by hanging out at the Pine Cove every day after work.

The Pine Cove Tavern is a cool little bar located right off of the 99 freeway. It is a small, dark, neighborhood bar that sits on top of the Pine Cove Liquor store. Once you enter the door from the street, you climb the stairs to enter the bar. Upon entering, there are windows all around the perimeter with tables that line the walls, which allows you to look out and down to out to the scenery outside as you sit back, relax, have a drink, and socialize with the other patrons. Nowadays it is a hang out for college students, people getting out of work on their way home, and the people who live in the neighborhood and surrounding area.

Back in the late 1970s and early eighties most of the clientele at the bar worked in some form of law enforcement but by the time I started going there in the mid 80s there were not quite as many. In talking to some of the ones that did still go there I was really surprised to find that most of them were really cool. This was in stark contrast to what most of my previous experiences and relationships with them had been, which, because of where I grew up, was one of dislike and mistrust in them. In seeing and talking to them in that setting and environment where they could relax and let there walls down, I discovered something that I had never realized before. Police officers are just like everyone else. They are good, hard working individuals who get up everyday, go to work, put in a day's work, and then come home to their lives. Of course their jobs are not like most people's jobs because each day that they leave their homes and go to work there is a chance that they won't make it back home. I began to see that they are not robots who are programmed to behave and act in a certain uniform way, be perfect upstanding, holier than thou, always on the job, model citizens at all times, no matter what the circumstances, which is always what I thought of them. They have the same feelings, strengths, flaws, weaknesses, and personalities that we all have. The main difference however is that with their jobs, those flaws and weaknesses can mean the difference between life and death for them and for all of us. My experience in going there allowed me to develop a newfound respect for those that used their badges to do what they swore to do when they took their oath, to protect and serve. At the same time however, I developed an even stronger dislike for those who used their badges to do bad things and to take advantage of the power that wearing the badge gives them. I found that although most police officers are good honorable people who deserve respect and thanks for what they do, there is still a small percentage of them that make it bad for the others. The racist and or criminal element within the force is protected and hides behind the blue wall making them hard to find. This made it hard for people in society, especially in the black community, to know which ones to trust. There were also those like Michael O'Sullivan who was a straight up racist and would express their feeling openly for everyone to hear, especially after having a few belts at the bar.

As James entered the door of the bar that evening, he could see that Michael was at the end of the bar that he always sat at and he could tell that he had already had a few. He could also see that another fellow officer that he knew pretty well was seated a few seats away from Michael, so James sat next to him, ordered a drink, and began to strike up a casual conversation with him loud enough for Michael to hear. James began ranting and raving, complaining about his job, having to work with a black partner, and having to work in a neighborhood with all blacks and Mexicans. He also said that he wished that there were something he could do to alleviate the problems with the minorities in the city. Of course it didn't take long for a combination of O'Sullivan's ego, his eagerness to recruit people into his secret organization, and his 4th round of gin and tonic to get James just what he needed. O'Sullivan, after listen to James's complaints, interjected himself into the conversation. He first challenged James telling him that he didn't believe him, and told him that even if what he was saying was true, if James were given the opportunity to do something about it, and had a chance to rid himself of his problems, he didn't think he would have the balls to do what it took to get it done. James, seeing that his opportunity had come much sooner than he thought, went right back at O'Sullivan, stood up to him right in his face, and told him that he didn't really know him, and that he didn't really care what he thought or felt about him or rather he would do anything or not. The bar got really quiet for a moment as the two men stood staring into each other's eyes, neither flinching nor saying a word, just looking, seeing if the other would back down. O'Sullivan cracked a slight, sheepish grin and said that he was only messing around with James, and told him not to be so serious. He said that he thought James looked familiar, and that now he knew that he'd recognized him for the academy when they were there together. James, of course, already knew this but acted surprised and said that he did remember him and that it had been a long time. O'Sullivan called the bartender over, ordered another round, and told him to poor James whatever he wanted and to put it on his tab. Seeing that the situation has seemed to resolve itself, the patrons in the bar settled back down and everyone went back to doing whatever they were doing before the slight altercation started. James would have to be very careful from this point on. He would have to get Michael to invite him to join his organization without making it look like that is what he was doing. This wouldn't be very easy however. Michael was very smart and very cautious about who he recruited and asked to join his organization. James would need to gain his trust, be invited in, and be in a position where he could find out as much as he could about the illegal activities that they and especially Michael were involved in without getting caught. If he were to act in any way or do anything that that would arouse either Michael's or anyone who was involved suspicion, they would not hesitate to take him out in order to preserve the secrecy what they were doing.

Michael began by making small talk with James, asking him non threatening things about himself, his family, how things were on the job, and other things like that just to break the ice and kind of get an idea of where his head was at. He didn't talk about himself much, or about his organization, and although Michael asked him a few questions about what they'd talked about earlier, he didn't really push things too much so as to arouse any suspicion. They sat and talked for a few hours, and eventually Michael again got back to where there meeting had began, the problems that James had been having with the blacks and Hispanics and the area that he worked in. He wanted to know what James's true feelings were when it came to working in an area that had mostly niggers and wetbacks as he called them. He wanted to know what James's feeling were on race, and how he felt in general about non whites. He asked James to explain his feelings towards minorities, and how he felt working in an areas where they lived. As James talked and told him what he thought he wanted to hear, Michael looked at him very closely and seemed to study his face and every movement that he made. He listened very intently to every word that came out of James's mouth, making him feel very uncomfortable. As uncomfortable as it made him feel however, he knew that Michael was doing this to see if he could detect any trace of deceptive behavior or actions in him, so he had to be convincing.

When James was finished talking, Michael began telling him the story about his father and it was a very telling tale that explained why Michael was the way that he was. It was basically the same story that our friend Big Boy had told me and Q about the police officer that had been killed in Oak Park back in 1969, but this time it was being told from a different perspective, that of a son, whose father he felt had been assassinated by black militants while he was on the job protecting and serving people in the community where he was hated by the folks who lived there.

Pete O'Sullivan was a decorated twenty-five year veteran of the Sacramento Police Department. He first joined the force in 1959 and quickly worked his way up to sergeant. He lived on his ranch in Elk Grove, which was a rural area at the time, with his wife and 3 young children, Michael, Lisa, and their youngest, Todd. Pete had grown up in the South, and been raised by parents who were both racist, and his father was a grand wizard of the local Ku Klux Klan in the small town in North Carolina that they lived in. Pete who was the last of 10 brothers and sisters, was raised to believe that white people were superior to all other raises, blacks were subhuman creatures who were to be hated and treated worse than dogs, and that he should always fight to keep the white race in its rightful place at the top of the hill, and blacks in their rightful place at the bottom. At first Michael resisted this, and once he married his high school sweetheart, he decided to move to Sacramento to get away from this sort of attitude, and to start anew in a new place. The seeds of racism are deep however, and once it is ingrained and drilled into a young person's mind at a young age, they are always there. What they choose to do about them and how they choose to respond to those things being in their heads, determines what type of person they will be.

Pete moved into his house Elk Grove in 1965, joined the police Academy, and upon graduation, was assigned to the Oak Park area. During the time, the Black Panther Party had just come into National Prominence, and had opened an office in Oak Park. Pete saw this as a revelation of what his father had always told him, so he decided to become a member of the local Ku Klux Clan to combat this evil organization called the Black Panther Party and protect the good white citizens of Elk Grove and Sacramento form them. Once joining the Ku Klux Clan, and working in he Oak Park, which was the home of the Black Panthers, and a predominantly Black and Hispanic area, he became obsessed with the cause of the clan, and tried to do whatever he could to further that cause by wreaking as much havoc and terror on the Black Panthers by any means he thought was necessary.

James listened very carefully while Michael was talking in a way in which it seemed as if he were actually there at the time, but in his heart, James knew that what he was saying was what he had been told by others because he was to young to remember what actually happened. Actually, no-one ever really knew what happened except the person or persons who actually committed the murder, and since the people who were originally arrested for the crime were found not to be guilty of it, no-one knows what actually happened or who killed Pete O'Sullivan except the person or people who actually did it. In Michael's mind however, it was obvious who'd done it. He knew it had to be the people who were arrested for the crime in the beginning, the McClatchy Park 4. He said that he knew it was them and that the only reason that they had gotten off was because the DA had done a terrible job at putting a case together against them and allowed them to get off on technicalities. He was convinced however that they'd done it. As Michael talked, James could see a rage growing deep inside, growing as he talked about how the 4 men, or niggers as he called them, probably went home and celebrated all night after getting away with murdering a cop. He became particularly agitated when he talked about how the murderers were still out there in society with their families and friends, never having paid for their crimes and sins, and for murdering his father. He said his father was his hero, and a hero to everyone, and that it wasn't right what happened to him and that someone should have to pay. James said that he agreed, and Michael ended by saying but hey, what can you do? James agreed and said, yeah, what can you do? With that Michael said he needed to get going, both men stood up, Michael said he hoped to see James around, maybe back at the Pine Cove some time soon. James agreed, Michael closed his tab, and left. James was a little confused. Maybe Michael had sensed something that he couldn't trust in James. Maybe he'd been too pushy and scared him off. Could he have ruined any chance that he had to get in with him? All he could do would be to wait and find out.

CARMEN AND LEXY

Carmen worked as an associate legal analyst at the Office of the State Public Defender and had become really good friends with a coworker of hers at the firm named Lexy Carlson. Lexy was white, single, and blonde, blue eyed. She was around 32 and had a perky chest, round bottom, and long beautiful legs. She had a carefree, fun attitude towards life and was considered to be a fun, beautiful and desirable woman. The men in the office were always trying to ask both her and Carmen out, but neither were into the White collar types, and were more into the blue collar strong handsome type guys. Both Carmen and Lexy began working for the laws firm at the same time and over the past year they realized they had lots in common, so they became good friends.

After telling me about her friendship with Lexy, I asked her if she trusted her well enough to let her in on what we were doing, and if so if she would feel comfortable casually asking her to help her find out what happened to her brother by trying to get close to the guy that she thought was responsible for his murder. Carmen was very hesitant at first because Lexy had become a very good friend of hers and she didn't want to ask her to do anything that might put her in danger. I was also a little hesitant because I knew that Michael was very smart and that he might figure out what was going on. This would put Lexy in grave danger, and possibly put Carmen in danger also. I also didn't know Lexy myself, and everything that I knew about her I was getting from Carmen, but I trusted that Carmen was a good judge of character, and knew who she could and could not trust, so that was good enough for me. So after talking it over for a little while, we decided that Carmen would ask Lexy to come to her house the next day to talk, hang out, have a few drinks and relax, and at some point in the evening we would talk to her about what we wanted to ask her to do.

So that next evening I went to Carmen's house at around 7:00. Lexy was already there, and her and Carmen had already started without me and both had glasses of wine in their hands when I joined them in the living room. Carmen made me my Myers and Coke and we sat in the living room and chatted for a while. There then came a point in the conversation when I asked Lexy if I could ask her something. She said sure, and to ask her anything. I then said that what I wanted to ask her was not really a question, but it was more of a favor, a favor for Carmen. She then said sure, but the tone of her voice was a little more hesitant and I could tell that she was trying to figure out what we were up to. I then told her that what I wanted to ask her, I was asking because Carmen trusted her and I trusted Carmen's judgment, and that if she decided she didn't want to do what we were going to ask of her, we would be trusting that she wouldn't tell anyone about what we'd discussed. At that point she began getting a little nervous, but she still seemed intrigued at the excitement and anticipation of what we were going to ask her. I then told her the whole story of Corey and Caesar's murders and our investigation and our suspicions about Michael and his involvement in the murders. I asked her if she would be willing to try to get close to Michael by going and hanging out at his hangout, the Pine Cove, and maybe trying to get him to talk about something that might help us get enough evidence against him that we could take to the police and get him arrested. I explained that we didn't expect her to sleep with him or anything like that, and under no circumstances did we want her to go anywhere or be anywhere with him alone. We just wanted her to go and hang out at the bar a few times, get to know him a little, and see if he gives up any information. She immediately agreed to help, and said she would love to help Carmen find out what happened to her brother. I asked her if she was sure, and told her that it could be a little dangerous, even though she were just going to be talking to him at the bar. I told her that he was a very smart man, and that if at any time she felt that he'd figured out what she was doing, she should get out of there right away. She said ok, but that she was sure she could handle him. She then asked when she should go to the Pine Cove, and I told her that he is there every Thursday and Friday From 6:00 p.m. until closing. Since in was Thursday, she said that she would go their the next day. Carmen asked her if she wanted her to go with her, and she said that since this guy was a racist piece of shit, it would probably work better if she went there by herself. I told her that might work, but to wait until they heard from me. I also told her that she couldn't tell anyone what she was up to, and she agreed. We then had another drink, and kicked back and relaxed the rest of the evening. Carmen was right about Lexy, she seemed to be a really laid back, cool, down to earth type of woman. She knew about sports, music, cooking, and all the important qualities that a man likes in a woman. I was very surprised that she'd never been married, but she explained that she was not in any rush, and that her mom had always told her seek and you shall not find, look and you will not see, but just be yourself, and love will find you. It kind of made sense in a way I guess. Before I left, I told them to not do anything until I contacted them first. They both said ok, but I wanted to make sure they heard me so I said it again, don't do anything until I contact you to do it, and again they both agreed.

The next day was Friday and all day that day at work Lexy kept bugging Carmen and saying that she was anxious to get started, and telling her that she wanted to go to the Pine Cove that night because Friday is the best night to go. Carmen kept telling her that they couldn't do it that night because I hadn't given them the green light yet, but Lexy was very eager and convincing, and told Carmen that she would just try to meet him that night, and that would be all. Eventually, after being hounded all day, Carmen agreed for her to go, but only if Carmen took her and picked her up afterwards. That way, she could make sure that she was ok. Lexy agreed, and they planned to go that night at around 9:00.

Carmen picked Lexy up at her house at around 8:30 p.m. and they headed over to the Pine Cove. Carmen showed her a picture of Michael that James had given her, and Lexy commented on how cute he was, and that it was a shame that he was an asshole. They both laughed about that. Lexy wanted to make sure that she would get Michael to notice her, so she wore something extra sexy that she was sure would get his attention. She wore a tight jean miniskirt, a low-cut blouse, and to put that extra touch on it, a cowboy hat and some cowboy boots. Carmen asked her if she thought she might be over doing it a little, and she said no, she knew what type of woman his type liked.

As they arrived at the bar, Carmen parked around the corner, Lexy got out, and Carmen told her she would be back in two hours to pick her up. They'd agreed not to tell me what they were doing because they knew I would have told them that there was no way I would let them do it without me being around to make sure everything went smoothly. They figured they would tell me afterwards once they proved that they could do it. I really wish they would have told me before however, and I would have let them know that it was an unnecessary thing for them to do, and it would only be necessary if James were not going to be able to get close enough to Michael. That is why I wanted them to wait, not because I didn't think they could do it.

But now here they were, and before Lexy went in, Carmen told her to be very careful, to not ask him too many questions that would make him suspicious, and then wished her good luck. Lexy said thanks, but that she really didn't need it, and that she would have him eating out of the palms of her hands within the hour. She then said she would see her in two hours, and walked around the corner, opened the door, and went upstairs to the bar. Carmen then drove off to visit her parents for a few hours while waiting for Lexy.

Once inside the bar, Lexy immediately attracted attention from everyone as she walked across the floor to the bar. Luckily Michael was there already, and there was an empty seat at the bar right next to him. She asked him if anyone was sitting their, and he replied yes, you, and she sat down next to him. The bar stools in the Pine Cove are a little short, so when she sat down her tight dress, which was already really short, went up even higher on her thighs, and Michael couldn't help but notice her gorgeous legs. He immediately offered to buy her a drink, which she accepted. He then struck up a conversation with her, which was falling right into her plan, or so she thought. If she had stuck to her plan and just gone there to meet him and to get out, everything would have been fine, but she wanted to prove herself to both me and Carmen, so she decided to try to ask Michael questions that she thought would get some answers that we might be interested in. What she didn't realize at the time however, is that Michael didn't trust anyone, whether it be his closest friend, or, a beautiful woman that he'd just bought a drink for at a bar. The first thing that he does when he meets people is to test them with various questions, and if he doesn't like the answers to those questions, or, if in talking to someone he has the slightest feeling that they are up to something, he will do whatever he has to do to find out what it is they are up to, and once he does, and it is something that he doesn't like, that person will disappear.

The two sat there for about two hours having what Lexy thought was a very nice and informative conversation, and at around 11:00 p.m. she said that she had to get up early the next day, wrote her number down and gave it to Michael. He graciously accepted the number and told her that he would be getting in contact with her really soon, she said ok and that she would be looking forward to it, and then she got up and left. As she walked down the stairs and out of the bar, she had a rush of adrenalin hit her, and she felt so proud that she had done what she'd come to do. She went around the corner, saw Carmen's car, and quickly walked over, jumped in, and they took off for Lexy's house. On the way there, Lexy excitedly told Carmen what she'd done, and everything that they'd talked about, and Carmen, while excited for her, began to worry that it all seemed too easy and that something didn't seem right. As she pulled in front of Lexy's house and tuned of the car, the two were about to get out when a black Chevy Camaro pulled up close behind them and two guys wearing ski masks, jumped out and quickly ran up to both sides of the car pointing guns at both of the women. Michael had followed closely behind Lexy when she left the bar. Close enough, but not to close as to be noticed by her or Carmen. Once he saw her get into Carmen's car, he quickly had some of his men follow them with orders to bring them back to him. The two men quickly ordered the two women to get in the back of their car, where another man was waiting with a gun in hand. They got into the car, and it sped off into the night.

SHOWDOWN AT THE RANCH

Big Boy would always call his daughter Korryn in the morning before she went to work and then again in the evening before he went to bed to make sure she was ok. That day, he'd plan to tell her that he wanted her to move back in with him and her mother until everything was safe enough for her to move back to her place. She'd just moved out of their house four months prior to that and had moved into a place right around the corner from UCD Medical Center where she had been working for the past year as a nurse. She wouldn't be happy about moving back with them but he hoped to convince her that it was the safest thing to do for the time being, and that once it was safe, she could move back to her place.

He'd already tried to call her several times at home that day but she wasn't answering. He then tried reaching her at work and they told him that she'd never made it in that day. It was around noon and her shift usually started at 11:00 a.m. so Big Boy knew something was wrong. He jumped into his car and sped off to her house to see what was up. When he got there, he knocked on the door and rang the bell several time but there was no answer. He began to realize something was definitely not right so he decided to try the knob on the door and it was open. As he slowly opened the door and walked in cold chills went through his body in anticipation of what he might find. It was eerily quiet in the house and he loudly called his daughter's name, praying that she would answer him, but there was no answer. As he walked into the kitchen and then into the living room, he could see that the furniture had been thrown all around the room as if someone had been fighting in there, or perhaps fighting off an intruder. He continued looking throughout the house, first her bedroom and then in the bathroom, hoping that he would find her there, but she was nowhere to be found, she was gone.

Earlier that morning Korryn was running behind and she was going to be late for work. She had been up late the night before hanging out with Q at his house. They'd been seeing each other for a while now, and they actually had gotten to a point where they really were getting serious with one another. She quickly showered, brushed her teeth, got dressed, did her hair, and grabbed her keys and headed towards the door. There was no time for breakfast, she was going to be late, and so she really had to hurry. Normally, she would do as her dad told her to always do when she moved out, open the curtains in the front window to look outside to see if it were safe to go out. He'd told her that she should do that because you never know what is going on outside before you go out there. So to be safe, he told her she should slightly open the curtain in the front window to look out to her porch and to the street in front of her house before she goes outside. Had she not been in a hurry that day, and had she remembered what her father had told her to do, she would have noticed the car that had been parked in front of her house since early that morning. She would also have noticed to two guys that were standing at her door for the past ten minutes and anticipation of her leaving for work. As they heard her opening the door, they quickly got into position on the other side, and as soon as she opened it, they pushed her back into the house and quickly shut the door. She tried to run away from them, screaming, and pleading with them not to hurt her, but they quickly grabbed her and attempted to hold her down to tie her up. She was a tough woman though, something that her father had taught her to be, and after being tackled to the ground, she quickly jumped up and kicked one of the intruders in the balls. She then punched the other intruder in the throat and ran for the front door. Thinking she was home free, she opened the door and went to run out to the front yard to scream for help. As she started to step outside though, she didn't see the third intruder that had been in the car, and had come up to find out what was taking so long. As soon as she opened the door and went to step out, he punched her square in the jaw so hard that blood squirted from her nose on to the wall by the doorway, knocking her out cold. The three men then quickly tied her up and gagged her, and after checking to make sure no-one was around outside, they quickly put her in the trunk of the car and drove off.

That afternoon Michael called James at around 4:00 p.m. and told him that he needed to talk to him right away and from the tone of his voice James could tell that something was up. He asked Michael if something was wrong and Michael responded saying everything was great and that he had finally gotten the last piece to the puzzle that he had been working on and that he wanted James to help him finally put the finishing touch to his masterpiece. James, not really knowing what Michael was talking about, but knowing what he was alluding to, reluctantly agreed to go to where he'd told him to meet him, his secluded ranch over in Elk Grove. Before he got off of the phone with him, Michael told James to make sure that he came alone, and when James asked him why, he said that he would be the only one who could understand what he had done and all the work he had put into his masterpiece, and that if someone else were to see it, it would be ruined and destroy everything. He said that would be something he couldn't bear and that he didn't know what he would do if that were to happen. James was very confused at this point. He didn't know what to think. Was Michael at a point where he had gained his trust and was now going to let him in on everything that he was doing and had done, or, had he discovered what James was up to and was he luring him out so that he could get rid of him because of everything that he'd already shared with him?

If he were to go he knew he might be taking his life in his hands, but he felt that he'd been doing a great job of fooling Michael up to this point and that he really didn't have to worry that he had found out what he was up to, so he got the directions to the house from Michael and told him he would meet him there at 6:00 p.m.. He called my house to let me know what he was going to be doing, but since Q and I had left to go to talk to Daryl, I wasn't there, so he left me a detailed message telling me about the call from Michael and letting me know that he would be going to meet him at his ranch and would come by my place to let me know what he'd found out later that evening. He the loaded both his primary weapon, a Beretta Nano, and his backup, a Colt Detective Special, the perfect weapon for situations when one thinks they will be searched because it is very small and easy to hide from detection, and it packs a deadly punch. He then left his house at around 5:30 p.m. to meet Michael at his ranch.

Elk Grove has come a long way in the last 20 years. Back in the mid 80s to early 90s a project was began to urbanize the rural area which is located south of Sacramento and north of Lodi and Galt. I say that it has come a long way because of the urban development that has taken place in the area over the last 30 years, and the influx of businesses, schools and many people from the Sacramento area, including my parents, selling their houses and building houses in the newly developed areas in Elk Grove. Prior to that however, Elk Grove was a strictly rural area, with lots of farms and ranches and once you left Sacramento and went into Elk Grove you were basically considered being in the countryside. The area also had a reputation of being a place where you didn't want to be caught if you were any shade of color other than white. During the time the Ku Klux Klan had a strong presence in the area, and this was true even as late as 1985.

I know this because I had first hand experience with them while on a picnic with friends in Elk Grove park one summer. As the sun began to go down and we were packing our things up to leave, we saw a strange glow coming from the other side of the park. As we made our way over to see where the glow was coming from, we were stunned to find that it was coming from a cross that was being burned, which was surrounded by around 40 to 50 people wearing the traditional hoods and sheets of the Klan. We quickly jumped in our cars and got out of there as fast as we could. So at that time, it was known that Elk Grove was not the place to be if you were anything but white, and that is probably why Michael decided to purchase his ranch there, on a road far out in the sticks, secluded and away from everything and everyone else, with the closest neighbor being at least 2 miles away.

As James drove up to the gate, it looked like a fortress. There was a couple of hardcore skinhead looking dudes parked in a car by the front gate. As he drove up, they shone their bright flashlights on his car. As he approached, one of the guys, a huge guy who looked to be around 6'3 and built like an NFL Linebacker or something, got out of the car and held his hand up for James to stop. As he approached the car, James opened his window and said that his name was James and that Michael was expecting him. The guy seemed to know that James was expected, and waived for him to go ahead through to the house, which was located way at the back of the 3 acre ranch. It was pitch black and James had to turn on his bright lights to stay on the road to the house. As he got to the house, he parked in the gravely area right in front of the house. He felt very lucky that the guys at the gate didn't frisk him to check for weapons and he considered this a good sign that Michael may be starting to trust him. When James got to the door, Michael greeted him and shook his hand as he walked into the house.

As they entered the front room, he offered James a drink. James said he would take a beer, but that he couldn't do too much because he would need to find his way back to the road after he left there. Michael kind of laughed and said yeah, that's true, but one won't hurt you, and then went into the kitchen, got a cold beer out of the fridge, opened it, and came back into the living room and handed it to James. After he handed James the beer James went to sit down and Michael stopped him and said that before they sat down he wanted to show him something. He then told him to follow him and they started to walk towards the back of the house. As they walked Michael said that he had finally gotten the final piece to the puzzle that he been putting together and that is was now time to finish what he'd started 8 years prior. He said that it had taken a lot of hard word work, planning and coordination to get in done, but that in the next room was the final piece something that he'd been doing for a long time, and something that he swore on his father's grave that he would do in honor of him.

James sat on the couch and Michael asked him if he was ready for his initiation into his organization. James said that he had been ready for a long time and that he would do anything that he needed to do to prove his loyalty and commitment to Michael, and to his cause. Michael told him that he was happy to hear that, and stood up and told him to follow him into the other room, which was a bedroom that was towards the back of the house. James had no idea of what was going on or where Michael was taking him, but he knew he had to play along and do anything that Michael asked him to do so that he could gain his trust and get the information that he needed to make a case against him. He knew that he was close and felt that if he could pass whatever test or do whatever task Michael was going to be asking him to do once they went through those doors, he would be in, and would perhaps get enough to bust him.

As they walked down the hall Michael asked James if he was sure he was ready to join his organization. James said that he was. He then asked him if he would be willing to do whatever it took to prove that he could be trusted. James was a little confused at this point, but he couldn't show any sign that he had reservations, so he quickly replied that he was willing to do anything to prove that he could be trusted. As they reached the closed door at the end of the hallway, Michael told James that once they went through that door there would be no turning back, and asked him again if he was sure he wanted him to continue. James said yes, but as soon as Michael opened the door James regretted what he had unwittingly committed himself to. There, with her hands and ankles tied to a chair and her mouth covered in tape, was Big Boy's daughter, Korryn. Michael had kidnapped her and brought her there to kill her, the final piece, as he would put it, to the puzzle and his twisted plot to revenge his father's death by killing the offspring of those who he thought were his murderers, the McClatchy Park 4. As James looked at him with a confused look on his face, Michael began to lay out his ingenious and yet twisted plot from its conception to its precise and ingenious and twisted end. James however, wasn't confused as to what Michael was doing; he was confused as to why he was brought there. Would it be to carry out the murder as one final test to show loyalty to Michael and to his cause, or to watch Michael commit the murder, or, had his cover been blown, and he'd been brought there to not only watch Korryn be murdered, but to share in her fate.

He had to be cool until he knew what was going on. After seeing Korryn he smiled and told Michael that this was great, but he still wasn't sure why he asked him to come there. Michael looked at him with a look both anger and disappointment, and after a few moments of silence, he reached over and put his hand on James's shoulder. James, a little startled by Michael reaching out to him, flinched ever so slightly. Michael, after firmly gripping James's shoulder for a few moments, said that he was surprised that James didn't know why he was there, and with his hand still on his shoulder, led him back out of the room, closed the door, and began walking back towards the living room area. As the reached the living room area, there, standing by the bar, with a drink in his hand was a man who looked oddly familiar to him.

Michael introduced the man to James as Stuart Green, a very close friend, and long time member of his organization. James reached out to shake the man's hand and as the man took James's hand he asked, been to Luigi's lately. A cold chill came over James as he now remembered where he knew this man from. It was the guy who we'd had the brief encounter with at Luigi's that day when he, I, and Q had met there a few months back. He'd recognized James at the meeting that James had attended the week before, and told Michael that he was a spy. He had to think quickly or his cover would be blown for sure if it already hadn't.

He knew that Michael already knew that he worked in the Oak Park Area, so he needed to try to turn the tables on this guy who was trying to expose him. He quickly asked Michael why he had this nigger lover here and that he'd seen him before, hanging out at a pizza parlor that only someone who loved niggers could hang out at. The guy quickly countered by saying that James was the one that was the nigger lover and that when he did run into him at the pizza parlor, he was with two niggers, sitting at a table eating pizza and talking it up like they were old friends or something. James said that he was there undercover, and the two guys that he was there with, myself and Q, were targets that he'd gotten in good with to bust a big drug dealer in the area.

Michael looked at James, smiled and said, well, there is only one way that you can prove to me that you are really down with us, and that is for you to be the one to finish the puzzle, and to put the nigger bitch in the other room to sleep, otherwise he would be watching them rape her and then set her on fire, and then he would be put to death as a traitor in the most painful way that he could imagine. He said that he would tie him up, cut his balls off, cut his tongue off, and then let him slowly bleed to death while his life's blood ran out in front of him on the floor.

The reason that James had been unable to reach me before he went to meet Michael was because Q and I decided to take a trip over to Seavey Circle after work to see if we could catch up with the fourth member of the McClatchy Park 4, Daryl (DR) Ridgeway, who we'd been told from a very reliable source lived there with his family, which included his wife and there their only child, their son Trent. If I'd been able to talk to him and he told me what was going on, I would have told him that it all sounded a little suspicious and that he should not go, or, at least to wait until Q and I returned so that we could follow him there to back him up.

It was going to be a little tricky trying to get in and out of Seavey Circle before dark, especially if we wouldn't be going there until after work, but we wanted to go there to see if Daryl could give us any information that could help us nail down our case, and we also wanted to tell him what we'd found out about Michael O'Sullivan and to warn him to be on the look out because we had a strong suspicion that he might be looking to do harm to either him or his family, and more specifically to his son.

Seavey Circle is a small housing development or project that is located in South Sacramento all the way at the end of Broadway just past the old Cemetery. The area is comprised or one and two story buildings that were built as affordable housing for low income families. The buildings are all bunched close together so as to fit as many people in the area as possible, and they all face inward and form a circle around the neighborhood, thus giving it its name, Seavey Circle. The Circle had always had a reputation for being pretty bad, similar to that of Oak Park, Meadowview, and Del Paso Heights, but it was different than those areas because it was a series of apartment complexes as opposed to houses, and it was concentrated in pretty much an eight block radius. None the less you didn't want to go there unless you knew someone, and even then, you needed to go where you were going, handle your business, and get out as quickly as possible. The same rules applied there as it did in the other urban areas in the city, you didn't want to be caught there after dark if you didn't belong or you didn't know anyone.

I picked up Q at his home at around 6:00 and we headed over to the Circle. It took us about 20 minutes to get there so we figured we had until around 8:00 or at the latest 8:30 to get in and get out before we would have any issues with the being there when we shouldn't be. As we turned on to the street leading into the circle there were lots of people in the entrance leading into the project and a lot of them didn't look like they would be very friendly if we were to try to ask them for help. Luckily we were given a building and apartment number from someone who knew Daryl really well, so we would just need to find out where the building was that he stayed in. As we drove down the street there was a slight breeze in the air, and there were lots of people in the streets just hanging out and chilin in there yards trying to beat the heat. Many of them, not knowing who we were, and not recognizing my car, stopped what they were doing as we passed by to check us out, many of them mad dogging us as kind of a warning to let us knew they are watching us and that we shouldn't be there. It is strange how most people who live in an area, whether it be a rich area or a poor area, look upon people who come to there who don't live there as intruders in stead of visitors. I always wondered why that was because most of the times the people who are going into an area that they don't live in are visitors and don't have any ill will or evil intentions in mind when they are going into a neighborhood they don't live in. They are probably either visiting someone or are there to try to get something that they need. I always thought if people be cautious with strangers but still treat them as visitors rather than intruders.

Luckily we were able to find Daryl's building without having to ask for help, but it was around 7:30 so we had to locate his apartment and talk to him as quickly as possible. We located his apartment and I parked the car in front. We quickly went up to the door and rang the doorbell. As soon as the doorbell rang the door quickly opened, and there standing on the other side of a screen door, was the hugest and buffest man that I'd ever seen in person. It was Daryl, and although we didn't really know him very well, we all knew each other from being around in the same places from time to time. I said what's up Daryl, introduced myself although I knew he knew who I was, and asked him if he had a minute or two to talk to us. As he stepped out of the door, he was so big, about 6"5, 270 pounds of pure muscle, he had to duck down to keep from hitting his head as he was coming out of the house. He shut the screen behind him, looked both me and Q up and down, and said, I know who you are, I know who both of you are, you got five minutes to say what you cam here for.

I held my hand out to shake his hand and he just looked in my eyes without moving a muscle. I looked at face as if to say we may have made a mistake coming here. I then brought my hand back and told him that we'd come there to give him a heads up on something that we'd heard about that he would definitely want to know about because it involved the safety of his family and more specifically his son, Trent. At that point it got quiet for a minute, and the look on his face turned from a blank cold stare to one of anger. He turned away from us for a moment seemingly hiding his face from us, and after a few moments with his back still turned he said, you got four minutes left. I started by telling him the background of our investigation, about, Corey's and Caesar's murders, about the rainwater murder, and how we thought they were all connected and were committed by the same person, a crooked cop.

While I talked, Daryl continued to keep his back to us, never moving an inch or saying a word. When Q said that the cop who we thought committed these murders was Michael O'Sullivan, the son of Pete O'Sullivan, the police officer that he and his fellow Black Panther members were acquitted of killing, he look up in the sky as if he were remembering and thinking of what happened way back then. Q hesitated for a few minutes to see if Daryl would say anything, but he didn't, so Q continued. He told Daryl that we were pretty sure that the reason that Michael was committing these murders was because he felt they'd gotten away with murdering his father, and that he was killing their children to so that they would feel the pain of loss that he felt when he lost his father. He then said that we had come to see him to let him know what we'd found out and to warn him of Michael's plans to go after his son.

Daryl still didn't speak a word. Instead he looked at the ground for a few moments and began to laugh. Q and I looked at each other thinking his laughter meant that he didn't believe us, but as he finally turned around, we could see that tears had began to form in his eyes, and in a low and somber voice he said that he wanted thank us for coming to warn him about Michael, but that we were to late. He paused for another moment and then continued on, saying that his son had been dead for 6 months. I told him that I was sorry for his loss and apologized for opening a wound that had to be still fresh in his mind. Q then asked him if he minded telling us how his son had died, and he said that his son had been set up and arrested for possession of cocaine. He was pulled over and an officer said that he found a large quantity of drugs in the trunk of his car, and so he was arrested and was awaiting trial. He said that his son was an honor student, and never did drugs or hung around people who did or sold drugs. He had just gotten a promotion in his job as an engineer with the Department of Transportation, and was on his way home to celebrate with his wife who was pregnant with their first child, when he was pulled over and arrested. While en route to jail, the two arresting officers said that he went crazy and went for one of their guns, and they shot and killed him on the spot. They were placed on suspension pending an investigation. Now where had we heard that before?

Once again we expressed our condolences to him, and told him to stay strong, and that we would let him know if we were able to bring Michael and his associates to justice. He shook our hands and told us if we needed any help, to let him know. As he spoke, he gripped my hand a little tighter before letting go, and said if we need any help of any kind, to let him know. I told him we definitely would, he gave us his number, and we left. It was around 8:30 p.m. just starting to get dark. We made it.

Q and I got back to my place at around 9:30 p.m. As I walked in the door I immediately saw that I had a message on my answering machine. When I turned on the machine we heard the message James had left for us. After listening to it I immediately knew that the shit was going to hit the fan. I wrote down the directions to Michael's ranch and told Q that we were going to have to go out there right away, because there was a good chance that both James and Carmen had gotten into some deep shit, and they weren't going to be able to get out of it without our help. Q said that we needed to get in contact with Big Boy as quickly as possible to let him know what's up, so that we could meet him at his house. We could then get over to Elk Grove as quick as we could. The reason that we wanted to meet at Big Boy's first was because even though Q and I had several guns ourselves, Big Boy had a wall safe full of different types of guns and knives that he'd collected while he was in the service and a member of the BPP and the Fruits of Islam, and he'd told us we could come by and use any of them if we needed them. He also said that he had guns that had silencers in case we were in a situation where we needed them, and this seemed like the perfect situation for that.

We quickly jumped in my car and headed over to Big Boy's place, but on the way there, we decided that we should get a little extra backup, so we stopped off and picked up Willie Boy. If there were ever a time when we needed his type of help, it was now. On the way we updated him on what was up, where we were going, and what we planned on doing. Of course he was down and actually seemed to be excited with anticipation of what might be getting ready to go down. As we got to Big Boy's he was standing in his front yard waiting for us. He asked us what took us so long, and said if anything happens to his baby because we took so long to get there, he would take it out on us. He looked at Willie Boy and said, "That includes your ass too."

Big Boy knew Willie Boy from way back, and the two had locked it up on a couple of occasions. I was only there once when they fought because Willie Boy had made a comment to Big Boy about how nice his daughter looked, and Big Boy took exception to it, even though Willie Boy didn't mean anything by it. The only thing is, Willie Boy, purely out of respect for Big Boy's rep in the neighborhood, tried apologizing for the misunderstanding, and Big Boy continued to push him on it. Although everyone who was there at the time could see that it was an obvious misunderstanding on Big Boy's part, no-one said anything to him for fear of what he might do to them. Also to be honest, the prospect of having Willie Boy and Big Boy throw hands was an enticing proposition to say the least, and would be something that we all would have paid money to see. The two of them squared off, face to face, two pit bulls getting ready to lock it up. It was going to be something to see and they didn't disappoint us. Willie Boy threw the first punch hitting Big Boy square in the jaw, a punch that would have knocked any of us out cold. Big Boy, having taken the blow full force, rubbed his jaw, looked at Willie, smiled and said, "That all you got, youngster?"

Willie Boy started to say something, but before he could Big Boy hit him right back in the jaw with a hard round house left, and then in the gut, with a wicked upper cut, again two punches that would have done the rest of us in, but seemed to have little or no affect on Willie Boy. From that point on it was on. Loud cheers came from the crowd that had grown to about 20 people, as the two of them rained blow after blow on each other's face and body for what seemed like an hour. Finally, after seeming to realize that neither one was going to fold, they both, bloodied, bruised and tired from the epic battle, looked at each other one final time, and simultaneously held their hands out to shake each others hand. Who was the winner? I can't call it. I say it was a tie, but I would definitely pay money to see it again. That was for another time though. We needed them to work together now.

Big Boy quickly took us to the back of his house and used some sort of remote to open the wall safe that had all of his weapons in it. I picked out my favorite handgun, a Glock G-26, Q picked out a Beretta 93-R, both of which had silencers. Willie Boy said he was straight with what he had, his two cannon 44 Magnums. Big Boy like to use his rifle, which he was able to fire in quick succession. I'd seen him do it before too. It was amazing to see, just like Luke McCain on the rifleman. He also took his high powered sniper rifle with the silencer and his night vision sight just in case he needed it. He said he was would need to be within 200 yards to be accurate with the rifle and be within 100 yards to use the scope. We then all quickly jumped in my car and we were off to Elk Grove.

We arrived at the street where the Ranch was located at around 10:00 p.m.. I shut the car off and we sat there for a moment to figure out a plan of action, but we didn't have much time to waste so it would have to be something quick and dirty. It was very dark and quiet, and from what we could see the ranch sat at the end of the street, which was basically a dirt road. The house was secluded and it didn't look like there were any other houses or properties for at least a couple of miles. We could see that the property had a gate around it, which was probably guarded, and it appeared as though there was only one way in and one way out.

The problem would be, how we get to the gate without being noticed, and if the gate is guarded, how do we get past the guards without alerting whoever was in the house or barn. We also had no idea how many people Michael had there with him and where they were. Whatever we were going to do, it would need to be done very quickly, and we would be going in blindly, and would need to quickly react to the situation and adjust our plan accordingly as things become clearer. In other words, once we got past the guards, we would just be winging it from that point on. It was a really shaky plan, but it was all that we had. We opened the trunk and got our weapons out. Willie Boy already had his with him. Big Boy said that he would go down the road first with his rifle and use the scope as far away as he could to see if there were any guards by the gate. He said to give him 5 minutes, and then we should start up after him. He said that if we started to receive fire or any type of resistance, he either was unable to get close enough to see his target, or he was dead, and that we would have to rush the gate to try and take out whoever got him before they were able to go and warn whoever else was there. He said that if there were no guards, or if he was able to take them out, he would whistle, and they could then make there way towards the gate. He then said the once we all got past the front gate, we should use the guns with the silencers to take out anyone that they saw other than the girls. I made sure to say that we should be careful not to mistake James for one of them also and Big Boy reluctantly said, oh yeah, and him too. I looked at him as if to say are you serious right now, and he just looked at me and said that he just forgot about him.

At that point Big Boy grabbed up both his rife and his shotgun and said don't forget, 5 minutes and that he would meet us on the other side of the fence if everything went ok. With that he began to slowly walk down the street, staying close to the side of the road which was lined by small trees on both sides. I looked at Q and asked him if he was ready to do this, and he said for sho, even though he looked a little anxious and apprehensive especially since there were so many unknowns about what we were about to do. I looked at Willie Boy, and before I could even ask him if he was ready, he said it seemed like it had already been 5 minutes. It had only been 2. He was ready.

All of a sudden the quiet was interrupted by the sound of Big Boy's whistle. He'd either taken out the guards or there were none. We all slowly began to walk down the road towards to ranch making sure to stay as close to the trees as possible. Once we finally got the gate, it was open and we walked through and went to the left side of the road, Big Boy, who had been hiding in the bushes that were on that side, stepped out from behind them with his shotgun in his hand. He had hidden the rifle in the bushes. I asked if there had been any guards at the gate and he pointed to the back of the bushes. I went to look and there lying on their backs were two skinhead looking dudes, one with half of his head gone, and the other with one with a huge hole in his chest with smoke coming out of it.

It was pitch black out there in the sticks. It was hot, sticky hot, and eerily quiet. From where we were standing by the gate, the only lights that could be seen was the light coming from the house, which was about 50 yards directly in front of us, and from a light that was coming from a window in the barn, which was around 20 yards to the right of the house. The grass, which was on each side of the roadway that led up to the house, was very high, around 4 feet or so which would make it easier for us to stoop down and use it as cover while we attempt to sneak up on the house. As I moved back over to where the others were, Big Boy said that he and I should circle around on one the left side of the house, and that Q and Willie Boy should circle around to the right side of the house, and we should meet in the back after looking in any windows on either side of the house.

As we began to move towards the side of the house, my heart started to almost beat through my chest, but it was not from fear. It was from the adrenaline and excitement of finally being here. Whatever happens, we were finally here at the end of this winding road that we had been on to find the truth about what happened to our friend, and to bring to justice in one way or another, the person, or people who were responsible for his murder. Big Boy and I quietly circled to the left side of the house and looked in the two windows that were on that side. When new looked in the first window we saw three middle aged cowboy looking dudes, dressed in levis, tee shirts, cowboy hats, and cowboy boots. They were all sitting around a table playing some sort of card game, drinking beers, and watching some game show on TV. The second window was to a room, and when we looked in that window we saw Carmen and her friend Lexy tied to chairs and gagged. Lexy looked like she had really been beaten up pretty badly, and looked to be unconscious.

When we met Q and Willie Boy at the back of the house, they said that there was another room on the other side of the house, but that there was no-one in it. Big Boy placed his shotgun on the ground and quickly went back to the first window on the side of the house where we'd seen the three men sitting playing cards. The window was open, so he quickly put his silencer back on his weapon, pointed his rifle at his first target, and fired, splitting his head in two. He then quickly shot the other two in the same fashion, shooting the third as he tried to run away in the back of his head, splattering his blood on the wall. He ran back over to us and said everything was clear in the house, so Q and I ran back to the second window where we'd seen the two girls. This window was also open so I quickly climbed in, untied the women from the chairs, and took the gags off of their mouths. I asked Carmen if she was ok, and she said she was. I asked if Lexy was ok, and she said that she'd been beaten up pretty badly because Michael found out what she was doing and beat her and threatened to kill her unless she helped him get me. I guess she'd resisted until she couldn't resist any longer. Carmen and I helped Lexy to her feet, and handed her out the window to Q. Once we go out I asked her if she could make it to my car at the end of the road. She said she could. I said to go there as quickly and quietly as she could, and once she got there, to drive to the closest house or store that she could find, call the police, and tell them that officer James Cool is in grave danger and in need of assistance. She asked if I knew if he was still alive, I said I didn't, but if she told the police that it was us out there and in need of assistance they might never go. She put Lexy's arm around her neck, I asked Lexy, who was barely conscious at this point, if she could make it, she said yes, and they began to head towards the car. Before they left however, I took Lexy's hand, looked into her eyes, and told her how much we all appreciated what she tried to do for us. She said it was fun, and we all quietly let out a laugh.

Q and I headed back to the back of the house where Big Boy and Willie Boy were. I told them that since we hadn't seen Michael, James or Korryn in the house, they had to all be in the Barn, so we all got our guns ready to go, and slowly started walking towards the window of the barn. As we drew closer, we began to hear a male voice yelling at the top of his lungs, and as we got to the window and looked it, we saw that it was Michael, and he was yelling at James who looked like he had been beaten really badly, with a gun pointed at his head. Michael had a gun in his hand, but he had it pointed at Korryn, who looked as though she'd also been beaten, and was tied to a chair. There were at least seven other men standing around watching, all of which had firearms ranging from handguns, to rifles, to sawed off shotguns.

Before we could think of what to do, Michael suddenly pointed the gun in his hand at Korryn, and as he fired, James jumped in front of her, catching the bullet in his shoulder. Big Boy, seeing this, didn't wait around any longer. He ran around to the barn door, kicked it open, and with his shotgun in hand, started blasting, shooting two of the guys who were standing around. They didn't know what hit them. The rest of them took cover. Q, with no regard for his own safety, ran into the barn firing his weapon as he ran, and quickly grabbed Korryn, chair and all, and attempted to get her to safety and out of the line of gunfire. He was able to do this, but in doing so he caught a bullet in his left leg, and he fell to the floor and out in the open. Seeing this I quickly backed up, got a running start, and dove through the window, and ran to help Q. As I ran in blasting, I was able to shoot two of the guys who were hiding behind a tractor, but in doing this I left myself wide open to the other guys, who all took aim to pump a few hot ones in me. As I grabbed Q and dragged him over where Korryn was, I heard three loud bangs that sounded like cannon fire, and as I turned around I saw Willie Boy who had followed closely behind Big Boy through the barn, standing there with his two 44 cannons, both with smoke coming out of the end of them. He'd taken the three guys out, including Michael. Once again I owed him my life. That was it, they were all gone.

I asked Q and Korryn if they were ok and they both said they were. Big Boy was leaning over his daughter rubbing her back as she sat on the ground holding Q's head in her lap. The crazy thing was, since Q had saved his daughter's life, Big Boy didn't seem to care. When I asked Q if he was ok he said he was cool, and motioned for me to come close so that he could whisper something in my ear. As I got close enough so that no-one else could hear what he said, he whispered, I told you me and Big Boy were cool. I looked at him, looked up at Big Boy, and said, yeah, I guess you are right, and we both started laughing. After making sure Q was ok, I went over to check on James. He said that he'd taken one in the shoulder, but that he would be ok.

As we all walked out of the barn door and made our way to the road, the sounds of sirens filled the air and we could see what seemed like 100 police cars flying down the road towards us. As they arrived, James made his way to the front, identified himself as a police officer, and slowly explained everything that had happened to the officers that arrived on the scene. It was over. We'd finally achieved what we'd set out to do, find and bring to justice, albeit Texas justice, the person or people who'd murdered our friends Corey Jenkins and Caesar Martinez,

That night, I was finally able to get a good night sleep for a change. It had been a long, hard, crazy day, but for once, my mind was free, clear and at peace. It was as if it had been exorcised of demons that had been haunting it for many years, and now that those demons were gone I could get on with my life. I slept so well that night.

I took the next week off, unplugged my phone, went and visited my mom, my family, and my close friends Q and James in the hospital. They were both on the way to full recovery and I was very happy about that. When I got back to work the next Monday my first appointment of the day was going to be a woman I'd never met, who had contacted me through Carmen's friend Lexy. Lexy had started hanging out with James, and through him she said that one of her friends had an issue that she told her I might be able to help her with. I'd only talked to her through James, and apparently she had an issue with a guy that she had a friendship type relationship with in which they both felt afraid and guilty about taking it further. So as a favor to Lexy for helping us, I agreed to have a meeting with this lady to see if there was something I could help her with in regards to her problem. Although I had encountered similar cases in the past, the guilt from the issue that keeps them apart is usually too big for them to overcome, and although they try to make it work, the guilt usually wins out and eventually tears them apart. I owe Lexy for putting her life on the line to help us though, so I set up a meeting with the lady for the next day.

After talking to Lexy I took a ride over to Q's house to see how he was doing. When I got there Korryn answered the door and led me back to the den where Q was kicking back on the couch watching TV. As Korryn left them room I asked him how he was doing and he said he was coming along and should be back to 100 % in a week or two. I then asked him how things were going with him and Korryn. He lowered his voice and told me that she had been smothering and spoiling him every since he got out of the hospital. He said that it was strange because in the past he would have been looking for a way to get away from a woman that treated him like that because he felt that they were only doing it to try to trap him. He said with her though, he felt that she was doing it because she was genuinely concerned about his well being and not about trapping him, and that that was different for him. He then said that he was confused about the whole situation and asked me what I thought he should do. I told him that he was sprung and that it sounded like he finally found his match and that he should just go with it. He told me that I was tripping and we laughed. He then said he would be up an around soon and that when he got better we should hang out and go fishing or something. I told him I would really like that, even though I really didn't like to fish. It wasn't the thought of fishing though. It was the thought of just being with my friend, hanging out, kicking back, relaxing, talking shit, and letting the world go by.

When I got to the office that Monday I had a very busy day ahead. I had a session with three couples scheduled that day, and I squeezed in the woman who I'd promised Lexy I would see that morning before my other sessions because I figured it would go pretty quick, since I would basically just be doing an evaluation. The appointment with her was at 9:00 a.m., so I started getting a session plan in place for when she came based on what Lexy had told me about her, which was very little. As I was sitting there going over my notes, my mind started drifting off and thinking about Carmen. Since my initial call to check on her after everything happened, we hadn't spoken to each other. It wasn't that I didn't want to call her, I really did, it was that for some reason I still felt guilty about my attraction to her, and even though I wanted to see her and to talk to her, and to stay in contact with her, I felt that I would not be able to control my feelings that I'd felt growing inside of me since the first day that I got in contact with her about her brother. It was like I was ashamed of my feeling for her the way I did because of Corey.

As I sat there my secretary called to let me know that my 9:00 a.m. appointment was there, and I told her to send her back. There was a knock on the door and I asked them to come on in. The door opened and it was Carmen. I told her that it must have been some mistake and my secretary thought that she was my 9:00 appointment that I was waiting for. She said that she was, and suddenly, everything became clear. She was the woman with the relationship problem where she and the guy had guilt because of their feelings for each other, and I was the guy. I really didn't know what to say at first, but I decided to play along. I asked her to have a seat, and I proceeded to go over my ground rules for my clients and asked her if she agreed to those rules. She said that she did, and then I asked her to tell me why she was there, and to tell me more about her relationship with this guy that she was talking about. She went on to say that she'd known the guy for years, and they first met when they were in high school. She then went on to say that she had always had a crush on him, but that he was a little older than her, and that she had a boyfriend at the time, a boyfriend that both she and he cared about, so she just kept her feeling for the other guy in check. I then asked her if she was sure the other guy also had feelings for her at the time, and she said she didn't know for sure, but she could kind a tell that he did. I asked how she could tell and she said because she had to walk past his house to get to her boyfriend's house, and it never failed that when she passed by his house, he was just coming outside for some reason or another.

At that point we both started to laugh. The conversation then got a little serious when she said that her boyfriend was killed, and at the time she thought that her world had ended, and that she was so lonely and miserable, and in need of comfort and support, and it was at that time that this other guy, who she thought was a close friend also pretty much abandoned her along with everyone else who thought that her brother was responsible for her boyfriend's death. She said that this really hurt her because she thought the guy was her friend and cared about her. I then told her that I was sorry that I'd done that, and that it wasn't just because I thought that her brother had killed Corey, even though that may have been part of it. I told her that the main reason was because I felt ashamed and guilty about how I felt about her, and that I selfishly thought that I should stay away from her to punish myself for having those feelings, never thinking that I was hurting her in the process. At that point she looked at me and said, well you did, and you hurt me very deeply. I then took her hand and said again that I was sorry, and that I would never hurt her like that again. I then let her hand go, and began to tell her my theory about how I thought her relationship with this person would go based on my theory and experience with relationships hampered by feeling of guilt, and I told her that it was my opinion that the relationship would never work out.

At that point she had a perplexed and sad look on her face. I then said that there are cases however, where it might work, if the people are willing to rid themselves of the guilt by realizing that they have nothing to be guilty of. She smiled and said she was willing to take that chance and I said so am I. I then called my secretary and told her to cancel all of the rest of my appointments for the day and that I would be taking the rest of the day off. I told Carmen that I knew this place that served a great breakfast and her if she wanted to go. She said sure and we got up and headed for the door. As we walked out, there seated at my secretary's desk, chopping it up with her, was little Cory, and as we walked in he turned and looked up at me and a big smile came over his face. It was Corey all over again, and his smile seemed to let me know that he approved of me being with him and his mother. We left the office, went and had a great breakfast, and spent the rest of the day hanging out, having fun, and enjoying ourselves without a care in the world.

When you think about it, it is ironic how all fathers have such an influence on their son's lives and who they become as men, either by being there for them every step of the way to manhood, or, by not being there and forcing them to make it there on their own. It is a fact that they must accept because they don't have any control over it. They can't run away from it because it's always there with them as long as they live.

Pete O'Sullivan went all the way across the country to try and get away from his father's influence over him, but in the end, it was already in him, and would be with him wherever he went, and it would eventually come out and make him just as bad as his father was, if not worse. The same thing could be said of his influence on his son Michael. James was also influenced and inspired by his father to become the police officer and human being that he is.

My father was my hero, and he will always be, not because he was perfect, he was human and had human weaknesses and flaws like everyone else. He was my hero because he didn't influence me to be who he was and to follow in his footsteps; he pushed me to be who I am and to make my own path in life. That is all any young man can expect their father to do for them in their journey to manhood and I will always be grateful for that.

WHEN I WAS JUST A YOUNG BOY

MY DAD WAS SUPERMAN

HE WAS MY HERO, BIGGER THAN LIFE

AND I WAS HIS BIGGEST FAN

HE HAD NO FLAWS

HE WAS PERFECT

SAMSON WAS NOT AS STRONG

THE WORDS HE SPOKE WERE ALWAYS TRUE

HE COULD NEVER BE WRONG

I ALWAYS FELT SO LUCKY

AND BLESSED WITH WHAT I HAD

OF ALL THE KIDS IN THE WHOLE WORLD

I HAD SUPERMAN FOR MY DAD

AND THEN AS I GREW OLDER

AND MY HEROES WOULD COME AND GO

MY FATHER'S FLAWS AND WEAKNESSES

SLOWLY BEGAN TO SHOW

BUT IT REALLY DIDN'T MATTER

I'M STILL

HIS BIGGEST FAN

HE'S STILL MY HERO AND IN MY EYES

HE WILL ALWAYS BE SUPERMAN

The Story

The coming of age can be a beautiful thing for young people. It can also be a difficult, hard, and sobering experience. It's August, 1980, and as another long hot Sacramento summer comes to an end, Perry Nelson and his crew are poised to serve notice to the Marks from the north side of the city that the real hoop stars reside on the south side of the city in The Park, Oak Park. Little do they know, later that evening something will occur that would forever change their lives, and in the blink of an eye, propel them from the immortal innocence of their youth into what can be the harsh realities of adulthood, the death of a close friend.

The endless days of summer are gone for good, and close young friends, once inseparable, go their own ways and follow their own paths in life; and though sometimes tested, only true friendships will remain and stand the test of time.

Seven years pass, and after a strange midnight call from an old friend, Perry's world is turned upside down, and he and his friends must take a painful trip back to that summer day in 1980. A trip that they must take to find out what actually happened to their friend and to find out why he was murdered in cold blood - and who had done it, things they thought they already knew, but that were now in question.

In order to find the answers, Perry will need help, and he must use all of his skills as an investigator to determine who he can and can't trust to help him, as he begins on his dangerous and potentially deadly journey to solve the mystery of his friend's death. Trust, friendships and loyalties are tested as Perry and his friends race against time to solve the mystery, foil the evil plan of the sinister villain, and try to prevent more murders of innocent people from occurring.

About The Author

I was born on the south side of Chicago Illinois in 1962 and moved to Sacramento California in 1966, along with my parents Lawrence and Cynthia Hobson and my older brother Bryan. After my younger brother Chris was born we moved to our own house in 1968. I then spent the rest of my early childhood and teen years in our house located at 3724 33rd street in Oak Park, on the south side of Sacramento.

I graduated from college with a BA in Finance and was married at the very young age of 22. After being married for 5 years, I divorced and then remained single until I met my wife Dolores at the age of 33. We have been together for 25 years, and I have a stepdaughter named Cynthia, who along with her husband David, blessed us with four grandchildren, Marcello, David or DJ, Andrew, and Alexis. I used all of my grandchildren's names for characters in the book.

After working for the State of California for 35 years in both Accounting and Budgets, I retired in 2017.